QUEST OF THE GODDESS

THE QUEEN OF GODS #1

LAURA GREENWOOD

Visit Laura Greenwood's website at:

www.authorlauragreenwood.co.uk

Cover Cyberwitch Press

Searching for gods isn't easy, especially when they don't want to be found.

A quiet life is what Hathor deserves now that fewer people remember her name. But when another goddess enlists her to the fight against spreading chaos, she finds herself out in the world for the first time in thousands of years.

Finding the other gods turns out to be the least of her worries. Somehow, she has to convince them to actually help her, and that's not as easy as she'd hoped.

-

Quest Of The Goddess is the first book in the Queen Of Gods Trilogy and is based on Ancient Egyptian Mythology. It includes a slow burn romance between Hathor and Amun.

GODS & GODDESSES LIST

Please note that this god list is a simplified version. Because of the span of Ancient Egyptian history, many of the gods and goddesses took on multiple roles over the span of time (as demonstrated in the story by Hathor's multitude of aspects). Some of the information below is specific to the Forgotten Gods universe, and is specified as such. I've tried to include all of the gods/goddesses who appear in the series below, but the list is by no means exhaustive. Please see the author note at the end for more information.

Amun – God of Thebes (former capital city of Egypt) and one of the major gods. Often combined with Ra to become Amun-Ra (they are two separate people in this series). Family: Hathor (Alleged consort)

Atum – God of pre-existence and post existence. One of the first Egyptian gods. Family: Hathor (Alleged Consort)

Hathor – Cow headed goddess who has represented many things over the Egyptian dynasty. Including but not limited to: beauty, love, sexuality, dance, joy, motherhood, queenship and sky. Family: Horus (Alleged consort or son depending on the dynasty.), Ra (Alleged consort), Atum (Alleged consort), Amun (Alleged consort), Khonsu (Alleged consort)

Horus - Falcon headed solar god, embodies the Pharaoh. Family: Hathor (Alleged Consort or Mother depending on the dynasty.), Isis (Mother), Osiris (Father)

Isis - (mentioned only) - Goddess and divine mother of the Pharaoh. Family: Osiris (Consort), Horus (Son), Nephthys (Sister), Seth (Brother)

Khonsu – God of the moon. Family: Hathor (Alleged Consort)

Maahes - (mentioned only) God of war. Family: Sekhmet (Mother), Ra (Grandfather), Ma'at (Love Interest in the context of this story)

Ma'at - Goddess of truth and justice, among other things. Family: Hathor (Mother according to some dynasties, but not in the context of this story), Ra (Father according to some dynasties, but no in the context of this story), Thoth (Consort, but not in the context of this story), Maahes (Love Interest in the context of this story)

Min - (mentioned only) God of reproduction, love, and sexual pleasure

Nephthys - A Goddess of many things, including childbirth, mourning, service (at temples), the dead, protection, healing, and more. Family: Seth (Consort, Ex-Consort in the context of this universe), Isis (Sister), Osiris (Brother)

Ptah - (mentioned only) Creator god, as well as the patron deity of sculptors, builders, and other artisans.

Qetesh - (mentioned only) Goddess of love, beauty, and sex. Originally from Canaan, she was adopted into the Egyptian religion.

Ra – Hawk headed god of the sun. Family: Hathor (Alleged Consort), Sekhmet (Daughter), Maahes (Grandson)

Rhodopis - the mythical figure from a legend similar to that of Cinderella. Her story is fictionalised in this universe in *Servant Of Chaos*. Family: Seth (Former Master in the context of this universe), Abu (Consort in the context of this universe)

Sekhmet - (mentioned only) - Goddess of war,

healing, and pestilence. Her story is fictionalised in this universe in *Daughter Of The Sun*. Family: Ra (Father), Maahes (Son), Ptah (Consort, Ex-Consort in the context of this universe), Fet (Consort in the context of this universe)

Serqet - (mentioned only) Goddess of healing and poisonous creatures. Her story is fictionalised in this universe in *Protectors Of Poison*. Family: Sed (Consort in the context of this universe)

Please note: Quest Of The Goddess is a fantasy based on Egyptian mythology. It includes an m/f relationship between Hathor and Amun. Gods/goddesses and their relationships towards one another may be different from mythology in this universe.

OTHER DEFINITIONS

Ankh - an Ancient Egyptian symbol of life.

Ba - the ba is part of what makes up the Ancient Egyptian soul. It represents the personality of the person.

Senet - a game similar to chess which was played by Ancient Egyptians. The aim of the game is to get the pawns to the Afterlife.

Waset - the Ancient Egyptian name for the

capital of the Middle and New Kingdoms. Otherwise known as Thebes (now part of the city of Luxor)

CHAPTER ONE

HISTORY HAD a weird way of remembering things. If I counted all the times something had been said about me that was wrong, then I'd be there for days. And numb to everything after. No matter what aspect of my life it was about, people had made up stories. My love life was the worst of all. They linked me to so many gods, I'd lost count. And the worst thing was that I had nothing to do with any of them. Especially not the one who was also referred to as my son according to *some* humans. I hoped they didn't think about it too hard, because even considering it makes me feel icky, and he *wasn't* my child.

Our lives had been seriously messed up according to the people who worshipped us.

I sighed and turned back to the loom in front of me. I wasn't sure why I'd bothered taking up such a boring pastime. Surely after a few thousand years, I should know myself better than to even try. It wasn't like I needed to do this either. No one needed me for anything nowadays. Though that could be because I'd been the goddess of so many things that no one knew what to pray to me for anymore.

At least they remembered my name. I knew more than one god whose powers had been weakened to the point of nonexistence because of how few people believed in them anymore. All they did now was roam the halls of the temple, unable to do anything other than exist. That was a slight exaggeration. They could love, laugh, and eat. And they didn't age. It was just their magic they weren't able to use.

"Your Eminence?" a priestess asked. She'd only just started serving me, and I couldn't remember her name.

"Yes?"

"The goddess Ma'at is here to see you."

I closed my eyes and groaned inwardly. Ma'at was....there weren't words to describe her. The goddess of justice could never leave things alone. As far as I could tell, she was currently on a mission to destroy Seth. Something no one had managed in thousands of years. I had to admit, he was getting annoying at the moment. And gaining power. Something about the chaos in the world made him stronger. And that was a problem. Then again, he did this every now and again. We'd all learned to ignore it.

"Send her in." There was no avoiding her. If I sent her away, she'd only come back tomorrow. And the next day. And the one after that. There was honestly no reasoning with her. I'd tried a few centuries back. She should have been the goddess of stubbornness instead of justice.

The priestess dipped her head and shuffled away.

I got to my feet and pushed the loom to the side. I'd have someone take it away later, but until then, I was stuck with it.

"Hathor," Ma'at greeted without a hint of warmth. We'd never been friends, but I also wouldn't describe us as enemies. More, indifferent partners in the same game.

"Ma'at," I returned. "To what do I owe the pleasure?"

"I've come to ask you to join our cause."

Ah. I was wondering when this was going to happen. I'd heard whisperings about it.

"No, thank you." I'd never been involved in any spats between the gods before, and I didn't plan to be now. Some would call it selfish, but I preferred impartial. If I didn't take sides, no one could act out about it later. To say most of us had been around for five thousand years or more, we could be a childish bunch at times.

"But Seth is gaining power by the day, if we don't do something about it now…"

"Then the same thing as always will happen. Osiris will go talk to him, and then he'll calm down and go back to plotting for the next two thousand years." These things always went in cycles. They were always the same and never ended any differently. Seth wasn't the kind of god who could be stopped. But he also wasn't the kind who achieved his goals, no matter how hard he tried.

"That's not going to work this time. His plans are already advancing a lot faster than they should."

"And what's he doing, getting a lot of minor deities on side and maybe a couple of gullible mortals?" That was pretty standard. As much as everyone liked to pretend, he was the kind of person who never varied the plan. One of the many reasons I didn't get involved. It was boring.

"He has Mafdet," she responded.

Ah. That was a little bit more problematic, though slightly confusing how it had happened. The god of justice was like Ma'at in most ways. To have converted to Seth's side…I had to wonder what he'd been promised.

"And what would you actually want me to do? Dance to victory?"

She gave me a weak smile. "You and I both know your powers are more varied than that, Hathor."

Hmm. That was true. Each time I was given a new aspect, I gained some kind of powers. So long as someone believed I was the goddess of that thing, I had it. One of the many strange ways our powers worked.

"You didn't answer the question."

"We need Amun," she whispered. "Without him, a lot of the others won't openly support us, even if they claim they will."

Ah. Now we were getting somewhere. "And what makes you think I have the power to persuade Amun on side?"

"You're linked to him, there must be a reason for that."

"You flirt with one god at a ceremony six thousand years ago and you just can't shake it," I muttered. "I don't know him well at all," I told her louder.

"What about Horus?"

"Him I know." Unfortunately. He could be an ass at the best of times.

"Can you persuade him?"

"What makes you think I'm even on your side?" I

asked. It seemed rude of her to just assume I was going to help her.

"That depends, do you like your life the way it is?"

That was a trick question if I'd ever heard one. Would she stop if I answered yes, or if I answered no? It was hard to tell. On the one hand, I was bored with my life. On the other, I wasn't convinced I wanted anything to dramatically change. I was quite happy just coasting through.

"I'll take your silence as a yes," she answered for me. "But that's not why you'll do this. Deep down, we both know you want to do what's right for the world. Your instincts insist on it."

Just as I was certain she intended, the mother-hood aspect of me rose to the forefront. There was an irony in that, as I'd never actually had any children, despite the many texts that insisted Horus was mine. But that just meant that I felt protective over all the mortals.

"That was a low blow," I said darkly.

"I have to do what's best for the world. Some-times, that includes using what I know about people against them." She shrugged as if it wasn't a big deal. If this was anything to go by, the rumours about her spending more time with Maahes than before were true. Only the god of war could have convinced her that manipulating for her cause was something she should do.

"Fine. I'll help." It might be against my better instincts to say that, but it would affect me in a bad way if the world really did fall into Seth's hands. He'd no doubt destroy all of the temples and carvings that depicted gods and goddesses who hadn't supported him, leaving us all powerless.

"I'm glad. If you could persuade Atum and Khonsu too, that would be great." She turned to leave, apparently having satisfied her need to get me on side and not bother with any pleasantries.

"What makes you think I can persuade any of them?" This was all of the rumours about the gods who were supposed to be my consorts at work. It was all rubbish. I'd never had anything to do with either of them before. And hardly anything to do with any of the others linked to me either. Nor did I intend for that to change.

"You're a goddess of beauty and sexuality…"

"And joy, motherhood, and queenship." Among other things. The list was hardly complete at those five.

"I think those things are less important, given the circumstances." She gave me a knowing smile. "Use what you've got, Hathor. They'll be eating out of your hand before you even know it."

That wasn't reassuring. Especially from a goddess who specialised in justice. It seemed wrong for her to be telling me to do things no matter the cost.

Ma'at didn't give me time to respond before leaving. Hmm. She really had just come for what she wanted. I shouldn't let that get to me, but I had to admit that it stung a bit.

The worst part was that I'd agreed. Which now meant I had to find a way to bring four gods over to the cause without a single clue what the cause was even about.

Great. I'd managed that one well then. I'd better start packing. The last I'd heard, Atum was on top of a mountain somewhere, and I knew that Horus hated staying at the main temple, so there was no telling where he was. So, not only did I have to persuade them, I had to find them first. This day just kept getting better and better.

CHAPTER TWO

PEOPLE WERE EVERYWHERE. Too many of them for my
liking, but I could already tell there was nothing I
could do about it. According to my sources, Horus
was around here somewhere. I hadn't wanted to
start with him, but he'd been closest to the temple
and a little part of me hoped he'd be easy to
convince.

Or that if I managed to deal with him, the others
would just fall into line. I knew it was a long shot,
but I had to do *something*.

A woman barged into me.

"Sorry," I muttered, even though she'd been the
one who crashed into me.

"Watch where you're going," she returned angrily.

My mouth fell open. Had she not recognised the
sacred emblem I was wearing? I didn't even realise

that was possible. It wasn't a surprise that people didn't worship us, we'd all come to terms with that years ago, but not to recognise and respect things at all? It didn't bode well for anything we were trying to achieve.

Now I remembered why I didn't come out of the temple much. I'd tried it a couple of hundred years ago and found it too crowded then. But now...

I shuddered. This is why I'd wanted to say no to Ma'at. She just lived in her own little world hoping that everyone would do her bidding. I would say that the joke was on her, yet here I was doing exactly what she wanted me to.

"Why would he want to be here?" I muttered to myself as I squeezed through yet more people and made my way to the bathhouse which thinly veiled one of Horus' temples. He hadn't even bothered to change the name.

I stepped inside, the bustle of people disappearing from around me and finally letting me sigh in relief.

"I'm sorry, madam, we're closed," a man said from behind a reception desk.

After a deep reassuring breath, I brought myself up to my full height. "Not to me, it isn't. Tell Horus I'm here to see him."

The man looked me up and down, probably

trying to decide whether or not he was going to throw me out.

"All right. If you'll just wait here," he said eventually. At least he'd recognised me. That was half the battle.

I wanted to argue with him, but decided against it. I didn't want to be here any more than Horus would want me here, which meant that ignoring his people would only make things more difficult for both of us.

The entrance was beautiful. If I had no idea what I was standing in, I'd have thought it was a replica of the temples of old. But it was more than that. This was an *actual* temple from years gone by. Horus had just had the outside of it changed to match the modern world. I had one much like this in another part of the city, I just hadn't been to it in years. There was no point. Some of my priestesses still saw to the upkeep of it, but as no one came to worship any more, there wasn't any admin to be done. Life certainly had become dull since the ceremonies and prayers stopped. It was so much better when people wanted my help.

The man scuttled back into the room, a cowed look on his face. No doubt Horus had filled him in on the details of who I was.

"He says to go away." The man didn't look up

from the floor. He definitely knew me now.

I sighed dramatically. "I was afraid he'd say that. Tell him I need to talk to him about Ma'at."

The man seemed unsure, like he didn't want to get involved in a battle of the will between two gods.

Smart man. In his position, I'd be avoiding that too.

After a moment of tense silence, he disappeared back where he'd come, no doubt to go and tell Horus my latest message. I just hoped this time he'd listen. When I'd agreed with Ma'at's plan, I hadn't intended for it to take up more than a few days of my time, even if the gods in question wanted to be difficult to find.

He returned at a run. "He'll see you now. In the receiving hall. It's..."

"I know where it is." I swept past him, trying not to betray the pounding beat of my heart. I didn't want for them to know how uneasy I was about this all. I'd never been the confrontational type, and this went against my nature. But if Ma'at's right, then I had to do this.

Cool air filled the temple as I strode through it, and I could see why Horus had never moved out of here. There was something timeless about it, and I longed to explore more and uncover the secrets hidden behind the stone walls. Plus, they were bound to have amazing baths here. Their front had to have some truth behind it or they'd risk being discovered.

"Beautiful set up you have here," I said aloud, not calling any attention to the way he was lounging over the seat and looking mighty smug with himself.

"What do you want, Hathor?" He studied his fingernails as if something of great importance lurked beneath them. He probably thought it did.

"Ma'at sent me." Not a complete lie, though it wasn't quite the truth either. She'd wanted me to collect up the gods she thought I had connections with, but she hadn't *technically* told me I had to go and get them myself. I could have just sent a letter. I would have done, if I'd thought Horus would reply.

"Yes, I've heard she's sticking her nose in places it doesn't belong." He swung his legs around and leaned forward, still not seeming that interested in what I had to tell him. I couldn't blame him. I didn't want to be in this position either.

"I'd hardly call Seth's plotting none of her business," I countered. "He's bad news for all of us."

"So you say, but he hasn't done anything to me yet."

"Yet being the operative word there," I pointed out. "He'll have it in for all of us. You especially."

He spun around in his throne, his feet touching

the floor for the first time. "And what makes you think he won't have it just as in for you?" He raised an eyebrow.

I lifted my hand and prepared to count off the reasons. "I'm beautiful, I'm smart, I'm non-violent, and I'm believed in."

"I'm two of those things," he countered.

"If you think Seth isn't a threat, then I don't think you have the right to call yourself smart any longer." I met his gaze and stared him down.

"Who said anything about smart? I was going to go with beautiful."

I scoffed. "I don't think Seth will be swayed by your *beauty.*"

Horus rose from his throne and made his way down the steps towards me. "We're thousands of years old, Hathor. Don't tell me even you haven't tried it."

I shook my head. Not in denial, there was no point in that. He was right, and he knew it. For most gods and goddesses, sexuality was nothing more than a word.

"You don't believe me?" he said.

"I don't believe in you in general." I wasn't in the mood for his games. I never was.

He clutched his hands to his chest, a fake look of pain flitting across his face. "You wound me, Hathor."

I barked out a laugh. "Please. I've heard worse said to your face."

"By people who I *like*," he stressed. "Last time I checked, that didn't include you." The venom in his voice would have knocked me off my feet. Or it would have done if I'd cared about what Horus thought. As it turned out, I didn't.

"I'm not asking you to do this because you like me," I pointed out. "I'm asking you to do it because it's the right thing to do." That was a slight lie. The only reason I was here was because Ma'at wanted me to be. It had nothing to do with whether or not I thought Horus would actually help.

"Then you've come to the wrong place. Go home, Hathor."

I sighed dramatically. "Don't expect me to come help when Seth is banging at your temple doors."

There was no point waiting for his answer, so I swivelled around and stormed from the room. Not that it would have any effect, I knew as well as anyone else did that all Horus would do was laugh at my retreating back. It didn't matter, though. I'd gotten the answer I wanted, whether he knew it or not. Now I could go back and tell Ma'at that her plan wouldn't work, and I'd go back to doing things exactly the way I wanted to. And no one would be able to tell me I hadn't tried.

CHAPTER THREE

I STRIPPED off my scarf and handed it to one of the many priestesses waiting on my return to the temple. They were a needy sort, always wanting to do some kind of service for me. At times, I enjoyed it. But most of the time, I hated feeling like I needed to be watched every moment of every day.

"Your Eminence?" my head priestess asked, curtsying before me.

"Is everything alright?" I asked.

"I'm afraid not." She swallowed loudly enough for me to hear.

Uh-oh. What was she going to tell me? I knew it wasn't going to be good. She normally blurted out whatever was on her mind and didn't care about the rest of it. I continued walking back toward my rooms, knowing she'd follow.

"One of your temples has been attacked."

I stopped in my tracks and spun around to face her. "Attacked?" I kept my voice level. It wasn't her fault, and I didn't want her to feel as if it was. Maybe some gods wouldn't agree with the way I ran my staff, but this was my choice.

"Yes, Your Eminence..."

"No need for any of that formality," I cut in. I didn't have time for her bowing and scraping. "Tell me what happened."

"Reports have only just come in," she said quickly. "So we're not sure exactly what. But there's a message for you, it's in your rooms."

"Thank you." I continued on my way, not stopping to greet any of the other gods I passed. None of them tried to strike up a conversation either. No doubt the thunderous look on my face was enough to put them all off. Normally, I was the heart and soul of the party, and I was careful to always appear approachable. It was part of what I'd become known for as a goddess, and normally, I wouldn't want to throw that away.

Right now, I didn't care. Deep down, I already knew who had sent me the note and was responsible for whatever had happened to my temple. Actually reading the letter was just a formality. Then I could decide how it was best to respond. At least, that was my theory.

My rooms were deserted when I arrived at them, and the priestesses following me quickly dispersed to their own space. Or maybe they went off to their lovers' quarters. I didn't care so long as they didn't bring any disrepute to my name.

The letter was sitting on the pillow of my bed, rather innocent looking for the disrespectful words it was sure to contain.

I unfolded it quickly, not wanting to make this last any longer than it had to. There was no way to make this easy.

My cobra slithered out from among the sheets, and I held out my arm to her, letting her twirl herself around my arm.

"What have we got ourselves into, Ura?" I asked.

She hissed, but that was to be expected, I couldn't speak to any kind of animal, not even the cows that were sacred to me.

The hieroglyphics blazed across the page told me all I needed to know. I stormed over to my bed-chamber door and looked around for the nearest priestess.

I motioned to her, and she rushed forward. Later, I'd have to remember to reward her with something.

She was only young, no more than seventeen, the common age to start serving under the god or goddess of their choice. Demi-gods often ended up here.

"Please tell Ma'at I want to see her," I said, ensuring that I softened my tone enough to not seem like I was angry with her.

"M-ma'at, Your Eminence?"

I nodded. "Tell her it is of the utmost importance and about the matter we discussed the other day." That should get her here on my schedule and not on hers. I could see the goddess of truth making me wait just to prove some kind of point. She was like that sometimes.

The girl dipped her head, then rushed out of the room.

I sighed loudly. Great, now I'd scared the poor thing. Oh well, it hardly mattered. A few nice words and a gift later and she'd hopefully forgive me. I had bigger things to worry about for the time being.

The time flew by as I paced back and forth, trying to work out what to do about Seth and him destroying my temple. The last thing I wanted to do was confront him, but there was a chance I'd have to now.

I reached out and stroked Ura's head gently. She leaned into the touch, enjoying the connection between the two of us.

"I don't appreciate being summoned," Ma'at said from the doorway. Her voice was a confusing mix of calm and reasonable, not a hint that she might be annoyed about me asking her here.

"There was no choice." I held out the letter.

She strode forward and took it from me. "We need to talk somewhere private."

"My bed-chamber will offer the best privacy." I gestured for her to follow me into the room, knowing she would.

I held out my arm the moment we were level with Ura's basket, and she unwound herself, slithering back into it and curling up. Satisfied that my pet was settled, I turned to sit at the small table that I kept in my chambers for this precise reason.

Well, not precisely because Ma'at was visiting, but in case of visitors I wanted to spend some private time with.

"Are his threats serious?" I asked, even though I was certain of the answer already. He wouldn't have bothered with writing if he didn't mean every word he said.

"As serious as he wants them to be. What are you going to do?"

"You already know the answer to that, don't you?" I countered, noting the small smile on her face that revealed I was right.

"I can't control you, Hathor."

"I wouldn't be so sure about that," I muttered under my breath.

"You have a will of your own, and just as much power and affluence as I do. If you really wanted to say no, then I wouldn't be able to stop you."

"Then why aren't you more worried that I will?"

"I know people." She shrugged, a slightly more relaxed Ma'at coming through than the one I'd seen up until now. "You might like to put on a front so that people think you're all about the relaxing and dancing, but I can see the truth. You'll always stand between your people and the things that want to harm them. Anyone that can't see that is a fool."

Which was why Seth had chosen to threaten them, and not bothered with me.

"Most people don't bother to look past the surface with me."

"I'm not most people," Ma'at replied.

"What do you suggest?"

"What do you want to do?" She adeptly turned it back around on me. Not for the first time, I felt sorry for Maahes. If the rumours were true, he had a lifetime of this to put up with. I didn't envy him.

"Seth needs to be stopped." The words were unnecessary, we both knew they were true. No doubt we both knew I was going to say them too.

"Then we need your consorts on board."

"They're *not* my consorts," I got out through gritted teeth. And they never would be. I didn't want to be linked to people I didn't know in the first place.

"Everyone else thinks they are."

"I think I'd have noticed if there were four men in my bed." I didn't even *want* that. One person there was enough for me. Sure, I'd tried out more in my early years, but it wasn't for me.

"Five," she corrected. "Ra is linked to you too. But we already have him on side."

I scowled. Why did everyone get it into their heads that they could tell me what my life was like?

"Fine, fine, we'll stop referring to them like that," she said with a sigh. My feelings on the matter must have been clear on my face.

"Thank you."

"But we still need them on side."

"I don't think I'm the right person to get them for you. Horus..."

"Is the least of our problems," she cut me off. "I know he can be a handful, but we're all certain he'll come around eventually. If we need to, we can get Isis to go talk to him."

I snorted. If they had Isis to call upon, then what did they need me for? I was nothing compared to setting his mother on him.

"Isis might be just who you need. That god is a brat."

Ma'at chuckled. "But still the least of our problems. We've heard that Khonsu has taken up residence in Cairo, and Atum is at his temple refusing to leave. But we have no idea about Amun. He's been missing for longer than we thought."

I tapped my chin. "Why do you think I can find him when no one else can?" My mouth felt unusually dry. I should have sent one of my priestesses away to get some refreshments for us.

"None of the traditional ways of finding someone have worked. We think it's time for the unexpected."

I raised an eyebrow. I still wasn't sure how that had caused them to come to the conclusion that *I* was their best bet to get these gods on side.

Not that it mattered. I could complain all I wanted, but I already knew that I was going to help. Seth had made this personal, and there was no holding me back.

CHAPTER FOUR

CAIRO WAS EVEN BUSIER than Luxor had been, and I hated it. I wasn't made for this modern life with all the people and the noise. But no matter how much I wanted to be back at the main temple, I was here for a reason, and I wasn't about to back down.

I looked behind me, half expecting to see one of my priestesses following. They weren't. I'd ordered them all to stay safely in the temple and out of the way of my mission. The last thing I wanted was for one of them to get hurt while I carried out Ma'at's wishes.

I checked the directions I'd been given and ducked into a side street. Just like I'd been told, a street stall sat at the bottom of it, a huge moon made up part of the sign.

"Gods," I muttered and shook my head. Khonsu

couldn't be more obvious about who he was if he tried.

I closed the difference between me and the stall, waiting for the old woman there to notice me.

"Hello, Khonsu," I said when she didn't respond, sitting on the edge of his stall and looking his glamour straight in the eyes. He might fool passers-by, but I wasn't a mere mortal and I wasn't going to be hoodwinked by this.

"I'm not sure who you're looking for, dear," the woman croaked.

I gave him a flat look. "That's not going to work on me."

"And why would that be?" An impish grin spread over her face, one that I had no doubt meant I was on to her.

"You know why that is. Can we speak in private?" Why were all these gods being so difficult when I went to talk to them?

The expression on the woman's face told me nothing.

I sighed. "This is about Seth."

Her face fell. "Come this way." She gestured for me to stand, and I did. Just in time, it seemed, as she hit a button and her stall covered itself completely.

"All right then," I muttered.

"This way." She ushered me towards one of the doors.

Now I was going to add annoying cryptic to the list of things I knew about Khonsu. Though admittedly, my list had been fairly short to begin with.

I stepped through the door and into a dingy room with a small wooden pallet as a bed, and an equally aged looking table. I couldn't believe he'd been living here. The place wasn't fit for a deity.

The moment the door was closed, the woman snapped her fingers and the glamour dissolved, leaving Khonsu standing before me in all his glory.

It was easy to see why he'd been using a glamour. The glow around him would distract anyone he came into contact with, and wouldn't be easy to explain to people. It surprised me he was like this. But then, I spent most of my time around sun deities, not those associated with the moon.

"Is there a reason you chose that glamour?" I asked him.

He chuckled. "People know what they want to see. An old woman like that is much more approachable than this." He waved a hand down his normal form.

"I suppose that's true." I paced around the room, trying to work out where he'd be comfortable with me sitting. With only one chair, I didn't want to take it away from him, but sitting on his bed seemed a little presumptuous on my part.

"Who sent you?" he asked.

"Ma'at."

"You're one of her priestesses?"

I narrowed my eyes. Did I look like a lowly priestess? "I'm a goddess in my own right."

"Those two aren't mutually exclusive." He shrugged and sat on the bed, which left me with the chair if I wanted to get comfortable. "Unless things have changed at the main temple."

"Not really." I had no idea how long he'd been gone, but unless it had been two thousand years, not a lot had changed.

"Then I stand by my point." He flashed me another impish grin, and I had to admit that it looked better on this face than on the one from before.

Despite my wishes, I felt myself warming towards him.

"I'm Hathor," I offered.

"I know," he responded.

"But..."

"I was teasing, Hathor. Everyone knows who you are. Your portrait is in almost every single temple I've ever visited."

I crossed my arms. "That's not true."

"If you don't want to believe it, then sure, it isn't true. But every god knows your face. Weren't you just upset with me for *not* knowing who you were?" His tone wasn't in the slightest bit accusatory, which only served to confuse me.

"Fine, I was upset." I unfolded my arms and flopped down on the chair. "But only because I'm grumpy. I don't like the world any more."

"Adapt or die," he responded. "That's what I've done."

"And it looks like you're living in hell."

"I don't know what you mean, my abode is charming." A smirk lifted the corner of his lips. I hoped that meant he wasn't serious.

"You need to come back to the main temple," I said. "And not just because I've seen the inside of this place."

He chuckled. "I wouldn't have thought you were capable of being so cruel. Is this to do with Seth?"

I nodded. "Ma'at is convinced he's up to something."

"That's been true since the dawn of time," he deadpanned.

"I know, that's what I said too. But she's convinced we need to do something about it this time. Apparently it's worse than the others? I'm not so sure." I shrugged hoping to convey that I thought the same thing as he did.

"Why did they send you? We've never properly met?" He leaned forward.

"Because we're linked as consorts," I admitted, throwing my hand up in exasperation. "But I wouldn't take it personally, you're not the only one I've been sent after for that reason."

A barking laugh came from him, at least he finds this as ridiculous as I do. "Let's guess, Atum, Horus, Ra, and Amun."

"All but Ra. They don't need to persuade him, apparently." And I was glad of it. Ra didn't have the best reputation, especially not among the goddesses.

"Horus is going to be the most difficult," he mused.

"You're not wrong," I muttered. "But you don't seem to be that bothered by the fact I've effectively been sent to collect you."

"I always figured it would happen some time. I'm just grateful that they sent someone nice to look at and not some priests to drag me back kicking and screaming." The left side of his mouth lifted up as if he kind of liked the idea.

Talking to Khonsu was certainly odd. We'd never met, and yet there was a definite familiarity in the way we talked to one another. It was like his *ba* connected to mine in a way that made me feel as if we'd been friends forever.

"Oh." I had so many more questions, but no idea how to word any of them. Or if there was any point.

He leaned down and searched beneath the bed with his hands, not watching what he was doing closely enough to make a difference.

"Aha!" He pulled out a small brown bag made of hemp. "You said we needed to go back to the temple, right?" he asked.

I nodded. "Is that all you need to bring?"

"It's all I have with me."

I frowned, trying to make sense of the man in front of me. Why was he like this? Most gods I met tended towards arrogance, but Khonsu didn't seem to care about any of that.

"You said you needed to get Horus to come back, right? We can stop by his temple on the way." Khonsu rose to his feet.

"We can try. I was there a couple of days ago." I pulled a face at the thought of returning.

"He might respond to me?"

"Why are you being so helpful?" Maybe Horus had ruined my opinion on what a reasonable god would behave like.

Khonsu shrugged. "I've been waiting for something like this to happen. I came to terms with it a long time ago."

"Oh." I wished I had a better response to that, but it made sense. I'd just expected all of them to be as resistant to Ma'at's plan as I had been. Which wasn't fair. Seth's influence was going to affect them all differently.

"I'm sorry, I never offered you any wine." Horror crossed his face.

"It's all right, we can have some once we're back at the temple," I said, rising to my feet.

"Sounds good. Shall we go see Horus?" The smirk on his face was unmissable. What was it about the other god that had him so excited?

CHAPTER FIVE

THE BATHHOUSE LOOKED JUST the same as it had when I'd been here before. But that didn't make it any easier to step back inside.

"Are you alright, Hathor?" Khonsu asked.

How could he read me so well already? I needed to work on my mystery, clearly.

"As I'll ever be. Let's just get this over with," I said with a heavy sight.

The same priest who'd been manning the front desk before greeted us with a cold smile. "Back again so soon?"

"Tell Horus I want an audience." I didn't have time for the small talk this time, not when Horus was going to test my patience once I got an audience with him.

"He says no."

"You haven't even been to ask," Khonsu pointed out.

"Horus informed me to tell you no the next time that you came to visit," the priest said.

"Tell him Khonsu is here to see him," he responded.

A triumphant smile twisted at my lips. Having the moon god with me turned out to be a good thing. I should have known the moment Khonsu offered no resistance.

"I don't think..."

"It's not your place to think." The glow around him intensified.

The priest stepped back in shock.

"I think you'd best go tell Horus that we're here to see him and we won't go until he sees us," I said sweetly.

"Yes, yes." He scampered out of the room, a terrified look on his face.

"That's a useful talent," I observed.

"It doesn't do much else. I only wanted to get the point across. I wouldn't hurt him."

"You don't believe in violence to get what you want?" I hoped he said he didn't. It would be nice to find someone who shared my ideas of peace for everyone.

"It doesn't strike me as the most obvious solution to most things."

A genuine smile spread across my face.

"Your Eminences?" the priest asked, breaking through my thoughts with his shaky voice.

"Hmm?" I raised an eyebrow.

"He says no."

I laughed lightly. "Of course he does."

"What do we do now?" Khonsu whispered to me.

"We go see him anyway." I set off for the same room I'd met Horus in before, ignoring the weak protests of the priest. He probably realised this was what I was going to do the moment he told us what Horus' answer was. I had to admit, he was a smart man. If word of him got out, then Horus might find several other gods making offers to his priest.

Khonsu trailed behind me, not saying another word.

Horus wasn't on his throne any more.

"He has to make this more difficult for himself, doesn't he?" I sighed dramatically. I had to go through with this annoying search, but that didn't mean I was ready to spend all my time going after Horus, especially when I knew where he was and this was all just some ploy to be difficult.

A doorway caught my attention from just behind

the throne. Knowing my luck, it would lead to his bed chambers. At least he'd probably be there, and think that I wouldn't dare enter them without permission.

He'd messed with the wrong goddess if that was the case.

I strode through the door, projecting as much confidence as I could.

Horus lay on his bed, a hand at a suspicious waist height. *Everything* was on display. If I wasn't so annoyed at him, I'd be impressed with what I saw.

"Eh-hem," I coughed.

He scrambled to his feet, grabbing a loin cloth beside him on the bed in an attempt to cover up.

"There's no point doing that, I've already seen it," I mused.

"Maybe I don't want you looking at me," he insisted.

I shrugged. "I'm the goddess of sexuality, you can't expect me not to." I smiled sweetly, but only because I knew it would annoy him.

Khonsu chuckled, but Horus ignored him.

"I thought you were the goddess of beauty," Horus shot back.

"I'm the goddess of a lot of things." The list was so long even *I* wasn't sure what the complete one was. I did know that sexuality and beauty were both on the list, though. As was motherhood. An odd combination at first, but I supposed sexuality and mother-hood did fall under the same category.

"That doesn't give you the right to stare at me while I..."

"It could have been worse," I answered, keeping him off guard with a gentle tone. I had to admit this was fun. "You didn't have anyone with you. Though perhaps I should be worried about that. Does no one want to share your bed, Horus?"

His eyes narrowed. "Plenty do."

"Then why were you alone right now? Or did you not think that someone else being here might have chased me away?" It wouldn't. Something I was certain he knew.

"What do you want, Hathor?" He finished covering himself, and I had to admit I was relieved by that.

It wasn't that his nakedness made me uncomfortable, I couldn't care less about it. But it felt uncivilised to be talking to him that way.

Khonsu's disappointed groan from behind me was so soft, I almost missed it. Interesting. I wasn't the one Horus should be paying attention to, then.

"You know what I want," I pointed out. "The same thing dear Khonsu is doing for our people." I waved behind me at the moon god. Though I could feel the amusement coming from him in waves. He was enjoying this. Yet another reason to like the man. Though perhaps that was more to do with his apparent attraction to Horus than anything else.

"I'm not coming back to the temple with you," Horus folded his arms just as his loincloth dropped.

I didn't look down, more interested in watching his face and the way his eyes darted to the god behind me. Interesting. Was there history between the two gods? It was rude to ask, even if they were eyeing each other up in front of me.

"It appears that your virility isn't compromised by me being here," I mused. "Maybe you don't hate me quite as much as you claim."

"I can hate you and find you beautiful," he snapped, his eyes darting back to Khonsu.

Oh no. His *virility* wasn't to do with me at all.

"You have no real reason to hate me," I pointed out.

"That's what you think." The muttered words were soft enough that I had to assume I wasn't supposed to have heard them.

"Come back to the temple and we can spend some time together," I suggested. "Then maybe you won't dislike me so much." A slither of hurt wound its way into my heart. I wasn't used to people disliking me. To most people, I was the epitome of charm and grace. Why Horus couldn't see that was beyond me.

"No."

"Horus..." I wasn't sure why I bothered. He wasn't going to listen to me no matter what I said. But with Khonsu behind me, I knew I had to try.

"The answer is no, Hathor. Just like before. You're not welcome here again," he warned me.

"What will happen if I turn up anyway?" I asked, already knowing there'd be some kind of repercussion. He wasn't the kind of man to issue empty threats.

"I'll get an amulet to guard the door. I'm sure there's something that will ward off beauty and sexuality," he bit out.

"I think you want a curse there," I quipped, not in the slightest bit worried. Most of the people who could cast that kind of magic were in Seth's temple, either voluntarily, or by force.

The more I thought about Seth and his power in the world, the more I started to wonder why I'd allowed myself to be as oblivious as I had been. He was a problem, one that needed to be stopped.

"Fine." I sighed dramatically. "I'll leave you alone. For now. But I will convince you to come join the rest of us. It doesn't matter if it takes an hour or a year. You'll be on our side."

Horus' eyes widened. "Is that a threat?" A deep vein of accusation sat in his tone.

"It's not a threat. It's a promise." I spun on my heels, leaving my words hanging in the air for him to think upon. I had no idea how I was going to persuade him, but I was certain I'd manage.

CHAPTER SIX

I RESTED my fingers on the pawn, not wanting to move it for risk of handing Khonsu the game. I was seriously out of practice.

"I haven't played *senet* in years," Khonsu said, echoing my own thoughts.

"Me neither, I'm rusty."

He moved one of his pawns a couple of spaces and I picked up the sticks to throw them once more and get the score for my next move.

I'd forgotten how freeing it was to sink back into the games of our own culture. With the modern world creeping in, some of the gods and goddesses had taken to playing more modern games. It was almost easy to forget the old ways.

"How long did you spend pretending to be an old woman?" I asked as I took my turn.

He chuckled. "Does it unnerve you that I did that?" He triumphantly moved one of his pawns off the board, getting it to safety.

"Unnerve is the wrong word. But I'll admit to not understanding the *why*."

"Maybe I don't understand some of the whys surrounding your life," he countered.

I frowned. "What would you like to know? I'm happy to tell you."

"Why don't you want to travel the world? We have fewer responsibilities now, you could take the time to really see things."

I scrunched up my nose. "The world is loud and full of people. It's not really my thing."

"I thought you were the goddess of..."

"Don't even finish that thought," I warned. Ignoring his words, I threw the sticks, rolling a four. Good, that would get one of my pawns past the houses and into safety. "Did you get to choose to be a god of the moon?" I asked.

"No."

"Then what makes you think I got to choose any of the things I'm the goddess of?" It made perfect sense to me. None of us were in any control of this. We just became the gods and goddesses of what people chose to believe we were. It was a confusing system. Mostly because it ended up with situations like mine where there was a long list of things one particular god was in charge of.

"I hadn't considered it like that. The moon has been part of me for so long."

I smiled and nodded. "As have my aspects. But sometimes, I want to be the real me, from before. The one that doesn't like spending a lot of time with people I don't know, doing things that I have to."

"Which is why you were on your own when you found me." He moved his next pawn, coming dangerously close to getting another one off the board and to safety.

I shrugged as I threw the sticks. "I'm immortal, it didn't seem overly important to take guards with me."

"Seth could have captured you."

"I doubt he's going to do that." I thought back to the threat in his letter and sighed. "He'll hurt other people in order to get to me. He wouldn't be foolish enough to kidnap me, it doesn't cause enough damage."

"Don't underestimate your value," Khonsu warned, moving yet another of his pawns off the board. One more, and he was going to win.

"If you think I'm in danger from Seth, then we need to act fast. Which means bringing Horus on side." I grimaced, trying not to think about my prior interactions with the god. He knew just how to get under my skin, and I wasn't sure *how* he knew how to do it. I'd certainly never given him any instructions.

"What about blackmail?" he asked, a thoughtful look on his face.

I stopped in my tracks, the pawn hovering in the air in my surprise. "You want me to blackmail a god?"

"Desperate times call for desperate measures," he attempted to explain.

"Even if it was ethical, I don't have anything to blackmail him with. I've barely spent any time with him ever." Which only made it more confusing that he hated me.

"Why does he hate you?"

I narrowed my eyes at Khonsu. How did he have such an uncanny ability to uncover my thoughts and voice them? Was it some ability connected to the moon that I didn't know about?

"I have no idea," I answered honestly. "I got the impression he wasn't my biggest fan about three hundred years ago, I've stayed out of his way since."

"Do you know anyone we can ask?"

"I doubt it. My best guess is that it has something to do with everyone thinking we're mother and son." I dropped my head into my hands and almost let out a wail of despair. How was I supposed to compete with thousands of years of pent up annoyance? Especially when we shared it.

"Ah, I can see how that might frustrate him."

"And me." I put the pawn down, having completely forgotten my move and realising we'd both lost track of where in the game we were. Other things were far more important.

Khonsu nodded, but then disappeared off into some odd train of thought. "What if you threatened to start telling everyone that you *are* his mother if he doesn't do what we want?" he suggested.

A light laugh slipped from me. "That seems a little unnecessarily evil."

"Or go the opposite way, and try promising that you'll tell people you're not."

I tapped my chin with a finger as I thought through the pros and cons of that one. "Do you think that will work? He doesn't seem like the kind that will fall for that kind of promise, especially if he thinks I'm just making it because of Ma'at's mission."

"It's worth a try, isn't it?" Khonsu picked up the *Senet* pieces and placed them back in their starting positions. It seemed like he planned to play again. Or he just wanted to do something with his hands.

I sighed deeply. "I suppose it is, yes." Though I

didn't want to admit that he was right. "We need Horus on side." More than I needed a little dignity.

"I can send a letter to him?" he offered.

I nodded. "Please do. With any luck, he'll arrive here tomorrow and then we can focus on the next god." Without me meaning to, an annoyed sigh escaped.

Khonsu cocked his head to the side. "Is it really that bad?"

"I have no idea how I'm going to manage all of this. It feels like I've been set up as a kind of joke."

"Ma'at never struck me as a prankster," he mused as he fit the last game piece back in place.

"Unless getting with Maahes has changed something drastic, she isn't," I muttered.

"Oh, so they're actually together? Interesting."

I chuckled. "No one knows for sure," I admitted. "But there's been rumours about it going around for a while."

"He never struck me as her type."

"I didn't think *anyone* was her type. Or that she'd end up with Mafdet because it was easy." Though even as I said them, the words sounded catty. Was it because I saw myself as in a similar situation to Ma'at's? I was alone, though I'd never considered settling for anyone to change that.

"So, Atum and Amun. How are you planning on

getting to them?" Khonsu asked, changing the subject.

"Can't we focus on one at once? Horus seems like enough work..."

Khonsu reached out and gave my hand an affectionate squeeze. "Let me focus on Horus while you concentrate on the others."

"I thought you suggested we blackmailed him?"

The god chuckled. "I was going to try honey before moving to the vinegar."

"I'm not sleeping with him," I warned. No one would be able to pay me enough to do that.

"I wasn't suggesting *you* did." There was an undeniable twinkle in Khonsu's eyes.

"Do you think he'll go for that?" I mused. "I mean, he did keep looking at you while we were there..."

"He did?" It was impossible to miss the hope in his voice.

Huh. I'd read that right then. Interesting. They'd make a cute couple.

"Oh, definitely."

"Well, I'll focus on him, while you do the others. At least that way we can both have some fun while we're at it." He winked at me.

I didn't even want to *think* about the fun he was planning on having with Horus, though I hoped the two of them enjoyed themselves.

"I doubt I'll have any," I said glumly. "Atum is an infamous recluse who thinks he's above us all..."

"Are you sure you're talking about Atum and not the big H," Khonsu teased.

I snorted. "He's not that big."

"That insult loses all meaning when I know you saw it," he countered.

I shook my head in bemusement. "Well, as far as I'm concerned, you're welcome to his big H. So long as he's willing."

"Oh, he will be."

"But I know where Atum is, so that's not too bad. Amun is the big problem. No one's seen him in so long that I have no idea where to even start." Of course, that was probably why Ma'at had delegated in the first place. She hadn't wanted to spend her time looking for him either.

"Okay, how about this. I'll go see Horus. You go to Amun's temple in Luxor and shakedown some of his priests, then we can go see Atum once we know more?" he suggested.

"It's as good a plan as any," I admitted. "But you're not going to come with me to find Amun?"

He scoffed. "You turned up to try and find me without any help, I'm sure you can find him too."

CHAPTER SEVEN

I REALLY WISHED they'd do something about the people. But no matter where I turned, there they were, snapping pictures and chattering excitedly in multiple languages about how much there was still left to see. It was unfortunate that one of my gifts meant I was capable of understanding them all. I assumed it was one linked to the motherhood aspect of me. I had to be able to understand all of my children, and that was what humans were.

I pushed through the crowd, trying not to think about how they were desecrating a holy site from years gone by. No wonder Amun wasn't here. I wouldn't be either if my temple had been turned into a tourist destination.

Once I was inside the main complex, I focused my search on the corners of the rooms, where someone was most likely to have hidden a secret door that led to the still active part of the temple. Perhaps one of the priests would take pity on me and let me in. Khonsu wasn't wrong about there being a lot of portraits of me. I could spot three from where I was standing now.

This happened at the temples of my supposed consorts sometimes. People used to worship me at them. I didn't understand why. I was always too busy watching over the people who asked for my help to ever find out. And now it was too late. It was one of the many things I'd never have the answer to.

"Your Eminence?" a portly man asked from beside me.

"Can I help you?" I responded, knowing full well that it was likely to be one of Amun's priests. No one else would know what to call me.

"I'm looking for Amun."

His eyes widened, and he glanced around, no doubt trying to make sure no one could have over-heard us.

"Come with me." He gestured me towards the back wall. That must be where the secret door is. I knew there had to be one.

Within moments, we'd disappeared from the busy tourist attraction and entered into the true temple. The walls were awash with colour, not having faded due to a lack of care. I hated what we'd had to do to keep ourselves secret, but after the people who worshipped us became less numerous, we'd had to do it. Some of the followers of other gods would have tried to kill us if they could. Of course, they'd have failed. We couldn't actually die. But that didn't mean they couldn't make us feel pain.

"Is he here?" I asked the priest.

He shook his head. "But I'm the High Priest for Amun. How may I be of service?"

I grimaced. What did I say to that? The help I sought wouldn't be the same if it came from anyone other than Amun, and I wasn't sure how much I could let his priests know without talking to him first. Some gods were particularly private about their affairs, and given that my only interaction with Amun so far in life had been a flirty conversation when we were both a *lot* younger, I couldn't make any assumptions.

"Is there somewhere I could leave a message for him?" I asked.

"You can if you'd like, Your Eminence," he said with a dip of his head. "But I'm not sure what good it would do. We haven't seen our leader in several hundred years."

I groaned. Of course, that was going to be the case. I was as guilty of abandoning my own temple as he was. Though I needed to visit to make sure my priestesses were okay and start repair work.

"I suppose he doesn't have much work to do these days."

"No, Your Eminence. This is only a smaller temple too, after the main one..." he trailed off.

"I know. I'm sorry about what happened."

A pang of sadness ran through me. Not at the loss of Amun's temple per-say, but at the loss of what Waset had been. As the deity of the capital city, he'd had plenty to do with his time, but that would have lessened the moment Waset became part of Luxor. I supposed he could have transferred his attention to the newer city, but that wasn't exactly how it worked.

Really, I was still surprised people remembered his name, given that his main temple, and the city he was the god of, were both things of the past.

"It was a sad day, but we live and prosper still," the High Priest assured me, more than a small hint of pride in his voice.

A genuine smile spread over my face. "As we all do. We've survived worse than this."

"Perhaps one day, Your Eminences will rule again," he said, a look of awe on his face.

My smile turned sad. I doubted that would happen. Our followers had turned from us before, it wasn't a new thing. We all still smarted from Akenaten's reign and his attempt to worship a god who never existed. But it had never gone on for as long as this, and I feared things would never change.

"Is there somewhere I can write a message for Amun in case he comes back here?" I asked. It was better to be safe than sorry, and I didn't want to have wasted a journey, especially when I could have used the time to check on the mess Seth had made of my temple here.

"Of course. If you'd like to follow me again?" He gestured for me to follow, and I did without question. I'd never been here before, and didn't know my way around.

For a smaller temple, it was so grand. Even some of mine didn't compare to the splendour of the walls, or the treasures hidden within this place. The humans of the world thought they'd found the most beautiful things that Egypt had to offer. They were wrong. Those objects still resided with us gods. And we cherished them more and more with each passing year.

"Here you are, Your Eminence. Can I get anything for you? Any wine? Refreshments?"

"No, thank you," I assured him. "I won't be here long. I have other people to visit."

He nodded, then stepped back, leaving me to

examine the scribe's desk in front of me. I took a deep breath, and pulled up a seat, before going through the steps I needed to use the reeds and pigments correctly. For quick notes, I often used modern methods of writing, but they still felt crass and unartful compared to the way a reed glided across parchment.

Perhaps I was too stuck in the past to appreciate the way technology had moved forward, but I didn't think so. With practised ease, I traced the hiero-glyphics across the page, making sure to put nothing in them that could get into the wrong hands. All Amun needed to know was that I was looking for him. I was certain he'd have heard the gossip about Ma'at going around, but he could grow his own conclusions about that and what I wanted.

I sprinkled sand across the sheet and let the inks dry.

"There. Thank you. If I see Amun, I'll be sure to tell him how helpful you've been today," I assured the High Priest. If Amun wasn't here to see it, then I needed to make sure he knew. Selecting the person to be in charge of the rest of the followers was always a tough job. I'd gone through ten years without a High Priestess at one point because none of the candidates had felt right for the position. But that meant a good High Priest should be commended.

"Your Eminence is too kind. Do you need help finding your way out?" he asked.

"No, thank you. I believe I can remember the way. I might stop and look at some of the wall carvings on the way, and don't want to keep you from your work." Which I was already very aware of doing. But in truth, I just needed a moment to prepare myself before going out among the tourists again. If only my magic included the ability to teleport. This wasn't the first time I'd wished that, and I imagined it wouldn't be the last either.

I made my way back through the temple, doing exactly what I said. It was odd, I never stopped and looked at the artwork on the walls in the main temple, it was only now I was here in one I didn't normally frequent that I found it interesting.

Without properly meaning to, I stopped at one that pictured me besides Amun. I had to admit, we looked good together, though I had no idea who'd decided to paint this, or why. I supposed it was an honour to have been linked to such a powerful god. And yet, I didn't feel grateful. I hadn't chosen this. It wasn't even a reflection of a part of my life I'd rather forget. This was something that had been decided for me by someone.

And Amun had probably agreed with it. Frustration welled up within me. When I *did* find him, he'd have some questions to answer. Because unlike Khonsu, I *had* met Amun before. And he'd been charming, older, more powerful. Though I supposed the middle one didn't matter too much any more. But to the young goddess I had been, it sure had.

CHAPTER EIGHT

"WHAT AM I going to do, Ura?" I asked my snake.

She lifted her head from my chest and shook it. A fat lot of help she was being. Then again, I wasn't sure what I was expecting. I *was* talking to a snake while lying on my bed, despite the fact I knew that wasn't going to help me with my mission.

"I have to go check on my temple," I told her. "That's not going to be fun."

"Hissssss."

I sighed and leaned in to scratch her head. "I know, you're right. I have to make sure everyone's safe and that we can start rebuilding. It's just, going there will make this feel so much more real." As opposed to chasing after gods who clearly didn't want to be found.

"Talking to yourself is the first sign of madness,

you know?" Khonsu asked as he sauntered into my room.

I twisted my head so I could see him, not even bothering to try and get him to leave. The soft glow around him intensified, bringing the sexuality aspect of me to the forefront. Not in a way that was attracted to him, just in one that could sense he'd had some *fun* with Horus.

"I'm not talking to myself," I pointed out.

"Ah, sorry." He dropped down onto my bed and reached out to scratch Ura's head. She leaned into him, enjoying the touch. She was a strange snake, it had to be said. But then, most of them were from my experience. "Is she giving you good advice?" he asked.

I chuckled. "Better than some I've gotten, worse than others. I have to say, her conversation is enlightening," I joked, but then regained some composure. "How did your meeting with Horus go?" I asked.

"Delightfully. He said I had hips like a cobra." He paused and looked at Ura. "I'm not sure if that's a compliment or not."

"From him? It sounds like it," I muttered.

Khonsu shifted, then laid down next to me.

"I suspect there'd be more than one person excited that we're in the same bed," he joked.

"And disappointed that it's not mine you want to be in," I retorted.

"I'm sorry, Hathor, you're not..."

"Your type. Trust me, I'm fine with that." It wasn't that he was unattractive. Far from it. Like most gods, he was handsome, well built, and confident. I actually couldn't put my finger on what *wasn't* my type about him. But I was certain we weren't a romantic match. "Have you always preferred men?" I asked.

"What makes you ask?" There wasn't any accusation in his voice, he really wanted to know the answer.

"Call it professional curiosity," I responded. "As Horus pointed out, I *am* the goddess of sexuality. My interest is easily piqued when it comes into question."

"That makes sense," he admitted. "To answer your question, yes and no. I've been with my fair share of all genders, as we all have."

"Fair point."

"But overall, especially in the past two thousand years or so, I've found myself more drawn to male companionship than women's. As lovers, I mean."

"I get that. I'm the same." It felt like the right time to admit it, though I couldn't say it would be a surprise to anyone. Most gods and goddesses were fluid when it came to who they chose to take to bed.

Mostly because we'd all been around a long time and the pool of choice was fairly small. Though I supposed it did get better when the demis who served as our priests and priestesses got added into the mix.

"But Horus isn't your cup of tea?" There was a hesitation to his voice that hurt me to the core.

"No. He never has been, and never will be," I assured him. "Besides, I always assumed it would be too weird and all I'd be able to think about was the fact some people think we're mother and son."

A shudder ran through me at the thought, causing Ura to hiss as I jostled her. I scratched her head in apology, and she curled back up, going back to sleep. At least, that was what I assumed she'd been doing. Despite the fact I *had* a snake, I didn't know a lot about them. But she'd been a present from a former High Priestess of mine thousands of years ago, and I'd treasured her ever since.

Khonsu chuckled, no doubt at the imagery I'd put in his head. "That would be a bit of a mood killer. I guess that means you don't want a blow by blow, then?"

"I don't want to hear about *any* of your lovers, but especially not Horus."

"I thought you were the goddess of sexuality?" he

teased. "Shouldn't you demand to know every detail?"

"If you want to talk explicit details, then you should go find Min or Qetesh, I'm sure either of them would be willing to help. I'm more interested in how people identify themselves and who they fall in love with." At least, that was what people had asked me for help with most often. They probably hadn't wanted to ask for help with pleasure from a goddess with so many different things to focus on.

"Suddenly I'm so glad the moon is a simple concept."

I snorted. "Don't even get me started on all the other things. I've lost count of how many people have prayed to me for beauty, but not given any parameters for that. Making them beautiful on the outside is easy, but even that fades if the inside is ugly." I sighed. For all the times I'd complained about requests like that in the past, I wished people were still making them. It would keep me busy and away from the boredom that had taken hold over the past few thousand years.

Which meant that Ma'at's quest was the most exciting thing to happen to me in a long time. Next time I questioned why I was doing it, I'd have to remember that.

"What did Horus say about joining us?" I asked. I

should have started with that, but talking to Khonsu about more personal matters had grabbed my attention too quickly. It had been a long time since I'd had someone who acted like nothing more than a friend around me. I liked it. Hopefully, I could keep things this way after Ma'at's plan had ended.

"The exact words, or do you want me to paraphrase?" Khonsu answered, a seriousness entering his voice.

I restrained the groan which wanted to escape. "That bad?"

"I believe it was something along the lines of *I could give him the most immense pleasure imaginable in this life or the next, but there was no way he would ever join you, even if the world was ending.*"

"Huh. Somehow I expected worse."

"I took some of the expletives out, if that helps."

"A little," I admitted. "But I still expected it to be worse."

"I'm sorry I couldn't do better," he said.

"Don't be. It wasn't like my mission was the real reason you went," I teased.

"Admittedly not."

I stared at the canopy over my bed. "I guess that means I have to blackmail him."

"Unfortunately."

I supposed that meant I'd have some time to visit

my temple before I saw Horus again. As the list of things I didn't want to do grew, I had to at least do some of them, and this one seemed like the one I shouldn't put off any longer.

"I can go with you, if you want?" Khonsu suggested.

It was a nice offer, but one I couldn't take, especially not if the two of them were going to continue sleeping together. I didn't want to cause any issues in their relationship.

"Thank you, but I feel like it's the kind of thing I have to do on my own. You can tell me how to get around his amulet against me, though."

He chuckled. "He hasn't put that up. I think he secretly likes the challenge you bring."

A small smile tugged at the corners of my lips. That was fair. There *was* something enjoyable about taunting Horus, though I wasn't sure what. It was best not to question it, or I might end up feeling like I couldn't blackmail him after all.

"I'll go after I've been to my temple." And done a few other things. But I didn't say that out loud.

"I can go before you and make sure he's in a good mood," Khonsu said in a tone laden with suggestiveness.

I smirked. "You can try, but I think his mood

would be ruined the moment I stepped foot in his temple."

"True. How did it go with Amun?"

I winced. "He wasn't there. I left a note, but I don't expect much to come of it." I filled him in on the rest of my trip to the temple. It helped to get everything off my chest, and oddly, it made me feel less like I'd failed.

"I hope he comes through. I've done some asking around about Atum too."

"Oh, thank you." I hadn't realised he'd had time to do anything more than visit Horus. "Where is he?"

"At a temple on the top of a mountain."

I groaned. "Great. Just what I need."

"We," he corrected. "I *am* going with you for that one. It's too long of a journey to do on your own."

I wanted to protest, but he was right. Plus, I didn't particularly want to climb a mountain on my own. It sounded lonely.

"Deal. But let's focus on Horus first." And hope that Amun would write back to me. I almost laughed at that one. As if he was going to. If I had to take my bets on what would happen as far as Amun was concerned, then I'd say that I'd end up searching the entirety of Egypt for him.

Potentially even the world.

CHAPTER NINE

A TIGHT BALL of anger rested in the pit of my stomach as I stood in the entrance to my temple. Rubble littered the floor, the remains of columns, walls, and statues.

The High Priestess of this temple rushed towards me, a horrified expression on her face. Perhaps I should have warned them I was coming. I hadn't thought about that.

"Your Eminence." She bowed low. "I'm so sorry for what's happened here. I was tending to the girls when they arrived..."

"It's all right, Anku," I assured her. "I came to check you were all okay."

"Oh." She blinked a couple of times as she tried to process what I'd said. Perhaps she'd heard of some of the other gods becoming angry when their temples were damaged.

I had more important things on my mind, though. This was the temple where we taught the trainee priestesses. Some of them as young as five. And unlike me, the demi-goddesses who served me could be killed.

"Is anyone hurt?" I asked. "I can send back to the main temple for some of Serquet's healer priestesses."

"Only Senebsima," she assured me. "But it isn't serious. Just a cut from where she was pushed aside."

My anger began to bubble away inside me. "What happened? I was only told that the temple was attacked, not the details."

"Why don't you come inside properly, Your Eminence? There's some wine and fruit we can put out..."

I shook my head. "I'll come inside, but save the food and drink you have for the journey to the main temple. I can't let you stay here."

Her expression warred between relief and regret. I imagined she didn't like the idea of leaving her own domain and entering someone else's. But I couldn't have them stay here. With the amount of damage that had been done, any protection spells would have been ruined, and if Seth's men came back again, they could risk being even more injured.

"Would you excuse me for a moment to talk to the others and let them start packing?" she asked, nerves filling her words. She didn't like being so unsure about what she should be doing. Probably because I so rarely visited this temple. I had to change that. If it was worth saving.

I nodded. "I want to have a look at what's been done anyway, then I'll know what to tell Ptah's builders."

"You're going to fix it?" Anku's eyes lit up. This was what she'd been hoping for, but she hadn't dared to tell me directly. My heart broke a little bit. I thought I'd created a good environment for my priestesses to work in, but it seemed that wasn't the case.

"If we can, then yes. We'll see what Ptah's priests say." It was the best I could do. Work on this scale would probably take decades to fix.

Seth was going to pay for this. It wasn't like this was my favourite temple, but that didn't mean I didn't care about it. I wanted all of my temples to be safe places, filled with laughter and joy.

And he'd filled this one with pain.

Anku disappeared, no doubt to find the other priestesses. With the small girls to account for, they'd have a lot of work to do in packing everything up. Luckily, I had enough space for them all in the lodging back at Karnak.

I paced the room, being careful not to step on any of the sharp pieces of rubble. Pottery shards littered the floor among the stones, and there were some patches of damp, probably caused by water or wine.

None of it was irreplaceable, unlike the people who called this place home. I was relieved they weren't hurt, other than Senebsima, and that she wasn't hurt badly, but it only went a small way towards quenching my anger.

All that being here was achieving was convincing me that Ma'at was right. Seth needed to be stopped, and no matter what, Horus was going to agree to help with that.

I stubbed my toe against a smashed statue. The head rolled against the floor, revealing my own face staring back at me, the nose chipped off in the fall. I hoped it wasn't some kind of prophecy for how I'd end up. I had no idea if I could be permanently maimed. I'd always wondered, but it hadn't been the kind of thing I wanted to try.

"They're all packing now, Your Eminence," Anku said, stepping back into the room.

"Good. Now, tell me what happened." I would

have had her sit first, but it didn't seem like there was anywhere good to.

She chewed on her lip, probably working out where to start. "We were about to start morning lessons. That's why I was with the girls and couldn't save any of this..." She waved around the room.

"I'm glad you were with them," I said, making sure to keep my tone soft and the anger out of it. I wasn't feeling any of it towards her anyway. She'd done the right thing in protecting the lives of the younger priestesses. I'd always want her to do that over protecting some stone effigies.

It wasn't like I was going to be forgotten any time soon, anyway, so it wasn't even that dangerous for my name to be destroyed in one temple. Even if I *had* been at risk, then I wouldn't have wanted her to protect me over children. I supposed I could have put that feeling down to my motherhood aspect, but I wasn't convinced. It seemed to be a perfectly reasonable response to people I cared about nearly being killed.

"Than what happened?" I prompted when she didn't continue.

"Three men came in, I think one of them was another god. They started smashing things and laughing. I took the girls to the back of the temple so they couldn't hear anything, and hoped they wouldn't come that far..."

The anger didn't want to be contained any more. They'd feared for more than their lives.

"Did they do anything to anyone?" The words came out low and cold. If Seth was standing in front of me, I could have ripped him to shreds with my bare hands. No one would be calling me the Goddess of Joy after that.

"No. They left after giving me a message. They said to tell you that Seth said to stop."

I shook my head. "Of course they did." I hadn't needed to hear his name to know he was behind this. No one else would have even considered destroying one of my temples. Even Horus, and he claimed to hate me.

I took a deep breath, surveying the damage again.

"I'm glad you're all safe. Please, make for Karnak as soon as you can. There'll be lodgings and positions waiting for you, and plenty of space for the children. Do any of them have families?" I asked. Some demi-goddesses were abandoned as children, others lived out in the human world until they stumbled upon us, but there were some who came from families already living in the temple compounds.

She nodded. "Three or four."

"I thought so. Send word to their families now. If

they wish to join their daughters, I'll ensure that there are rooms supplied for them. If they need me to speak to one of the other gods on their behalf, let me know, and it will be arranged."

Her eyes widened. Perhaps she hadn't expected me to suggest any of that. "Thank you, Your Eminence, I know the families will be more than grateful."

"They don't need to be. It's only right for families to be kept together. The girls have been through enough." I pushed the thoughts to the side before I let my anger get the better of me.

"I'll see it done," she promised.

"Thank you, Anku. Please, send word when you're at Karnak and we'll work out your position among my household. I promise it won't be a demotion, but I don't know how long this will take to rebuild, and we need to find a way to continue the girls' education." She was a good High Priestess, and they were hard to come by. The last thing I wanted to happen was for her to think I didn't care about that once she was under the management of her counterpart at Karnak.

"Thank you." She dipped her head.

"I need to go see Ptah about the damage here, but if you need anything, please let me know." That was a slight lie. I wasn't going to see the creator god straight away, I had other things to do first.

Including getting ready for a showdown with Horus. But I wasn't about to tell her about the inner workings of my day. She had enough to worry about with moving everyone.

"Thank you for everything you've done," I assured her before I left. I refused to become one of those goddesses who no longer cared about the people who served her, and if the past few days had taught me anything, it was that I was starting to become one.

Now was as good a time as any to change that.

CHAPTER TEN

I LET the linen bath cloth drop to the floor now it had done the job of drying me. Perhaps I should have gone straight to Horus' temple and demanded he helped against Seth, but instead, I thought it was better to come back to Karnak first and take a bath to calm myself. The last thing I wanted to do was ruin any chance of convincing him by acting in anger rather than rationally.

"I've heard you're looking for me," a male voice said from behind me.

I twirled around to see who was in my room. Ura reacted to his voice, uncoiling herself and hissing, her hood flaring in a sudden show of aggression. She was a good snake,, even if I'd never taught her to protect me. I wasn't complaining.

The question of who he was died on my tongue

as I took in the tall man standing in my bed chambers. Unlike with Horus and Khonsu, a bolt of desire passed through me. Potentially from the broad set of his shoulders, or from the way he seemed to be drinking in every inch of my naked body with his eyes.

Ah. Right. I should put on some clothes.

Instead of calling him out on it, I turned to where I'd laid out new clothes before my bath, and sauntered over, making sure to swing my hips a little more than usual as I did.

If he thought he'd get the upper hand by turning up in my bed-chamber unexpectedly, then he had another thing coming.

"What do you want, Amun?" I asked as I started to get dressed. Slowly. I wanted to make the most of the way he was looking at me. I hadn't felt this desired in a long time, and even if I wasn't going to act on it, I would enjoy the moment.

I snapped cuffs of gold around my wrists, before putting my collar in place. Technically, I should have left the beaded necklace for last, but that wouldn't produce the desired effect.

He cleared his throat. "Right now, I'm hoping your dress will burst into flames."

I chuckled. "I don't think that's part of either of

our talents." I picked it up, and slid it over my head. Slowly.

"I could learn another one just for this," he promised.

"That's not how it works." I tugged the material into place so it hugged my curves. It turned out that there was no change in the way he looked at me once I was covered.

"Unfortunately, not."

"You also didn't come here to see me get dressed," I pointed out.

"I came because you left this for me." He held up my letter, pushing away from the door.

"I did," I admitted. "But that doesn't explain why you felt the need to sneak past my priestesses and hide in my bed-chamber while I was in the bath."

I stalked towards him, trying to get the measure of him while wanting to be closer at the same time.

Ura hissed.

"Down," I commanded.

She turned her head towards me, as if to check I was giving the command I meant to, but then coiled back into her position on the bed.

"Are you always that good with snakes?" he asked, an impish smile on his face.

"Only big ones."

"I'm glad to hear it." His words came out a little

husky, probably because we were so close we were almost touching.

"What are you doing in my room?" I repeated.

"I told you..."

"My letter, yes. That's why you've come to see me, not why you've sneaked into my room and...what were you even planning on doing when you got in here?"

"Kiss you?" he suggested.

I had to admit there was a part of me which was tempted, but I knew better than that.

I stepped back, putting some much needed distance between us. "I don't kiss men I've just met."

"We met before..."

"Once. Six thousand years ago." Ish. I wasn't sure of the exact date. "And if it's been that long, then you need to reacquaint yourself," I added.

"But after I do that, I can kiss you? Good to know," he teased.

I crossed my arms. "Maybe. But it'll take more than a conversation."

"I like my chances, then. I can be very persuasive." Amun winked at me. Actually winked.

"And I can be very stubborn," I countered.

"Isn't that what makes it more fun?" he asked.

"Are you always this infuriating?"

"Only with people I like."

Despite myself, I let out a small laugh. "Then I dread to think how you are with people you don't."

"If you want to find out, I can name a couple and you can see if they'll come over," he suggested with a shrug.

I moved away from him and over to the bronze mirror set up in front of my cosmetics. I didn't need any, not for a conversation with Amun and then going to see Ra, but I needed to do *something* with my hands lest I start using them to touch him.

"I'll pass, thanks."

"As you wish."

"So, where have you been?" I asked. "No one seemed to have any clue where I could find you." And I was surprised he'd even turned up. I wondered what about my note had convinced him.

"Ah, yes. No one knowing a thing, just the way I like it."

"You're not going to tell me, are you?" I picked up a bottle of perfume and dabbed some onto my neck slowly.

He cleared his throat, but I knew it wasn't anything to do with getting my attention. I was affecting him, and we both knew it. Which was good, because I wasn't immune to his charms either.

"I don't see any reason to."

"What if I want to find you again?" And somehow, I knew I'd need to. He wasn't like Horus, that much was clear, but that didn't mean he wouldn't need persuading.

"Then you know where to leave a message."

I glanced over to the god, unable to resist. His eyes sparkled with promise, like he thought of this as a game of *Senet* and it was a piece he wanted to play. I wasn't going to fall for that one. I was a goddess myself, and no one would treat me like that.

"No, thank you. I think I'll choose to go without seeing you again." I turned back to the mirror and started to line my eyes. It didn't take much concentration, not when I'd been doing it the same way for so long, but it gave me something to *do* that wasn't stare at him.

But it didn't stop me from being aware of Amun's movements across the room. He stepped up behind me, the heat of his body radiating from him and warming me. He moved even closer, and it was all I could do to stop myself from pushing back into him. No one had affected me this way in a long time, and I had no explanation for it. But that didn't mean I had to do anything about it. At least not until I knew *more* about the god bringing out those feelings in me.

Our eyes met in the mirror, and it was impossible to miss the burning desire in his.

I set down my eye liner, and waited for him to

make a move. If he was trying to get the upper hand by doing this, then he was going to have another thing coming. The last thing I intended to do was let him have it.

He leaned forward, his arm crowding me against my cosmetics table. If I turned, we'd be so close that I was certain we'd kiss. Instead, I made do with the slight hitch in my breath as he leaned closer.

"You can use this," he whispered in my ear.

I let my gaze drop to the table where a small silver ankh lay.

"You can't...." I started, but he was already out of the door.

I had no idea how he'd moved so fast, as far as I knew, he didn't possess any gifts which would make him that way. A sigh escaped me. I wasn't sure *what* I'd expected from him, but leaving a sacred ankh hadn't been one of them. How was I supposed to use it to contact him? I had no idea they could do that. Perhaps this one was spelled?

But why? Was it so he could keep track of all his lovers?

I shook my head, not wanting to entertain those thoughts. Despite knowing better, I reached out and touched it. The smooth metal was warm, probably because it had been next to his skin. I closed my hand around it, then slipped it into the pocket of my dress.

Which was when I realised I'd forgotten to even mention the fight against Seth to him. Something I hoped Ma'at wouldn't find out, given that she seemed to think there was some kind of time crunch to all of this.

CHAPTER ELEVEN

FOR SOME REASON, going to Ma'at's chambers was more nerve wracking than visiting Horus, or having Amun turn up in my bedchamber unannounced. Perhaps because she was scarier than both of them combined. I'd never considered that about her before, which seemed silly, given that she fed the hearts of sinners to a demon if they failed her test to enter the afterlife.

"Your Eminence, come this way," one of her priestesses said as I entered the room.

I smiled at her, though I was certain the gesture didn't reach my eyes.

She led me through the main chambers, and through a set of ornate doors. The trickle of water reached my ears as we walked among a series of pools, each one with beautiful decorations and sweet perfumes lifting up from them. Why hadn't I thought of having a room like this built? It was beautiful, and calming.

While none of the pools were deep enough to have been a bath, there were small seats by them for people to sit on while they dangled their feet into the cool water. It almost made meeting Ma'at worth it.

"Hathor is here, Your Eminence," the priestess said as she drew back one of the gauzy curtains to reveal Ma'at sitting by a pool and reading from a couple of scrolls.

"Thank you, Edrice," she said. "Can you make sure we're not disturbed?"

The priestess dipped her head. "Of course."

"Please, take a seat." Ma'at indicated to one of the empty benches. I threw a longing look at the pools, but curbed my desire to dip my feet in.

Instead, I sat down, focusing on the conversation that was to come. No doubt it would be at least a little uncomfortable, given that Ma'at would want to know about my progress with the other gods. And that was lackluster at best.

"Would you like some fruit and wine?" she asked.

I shook my head. No part of me intended to be here long. If I took refreshments, that would only extend the time in her company, and I wasn't willing to do that. I didn't dislike her, per-say, but we also weren't friends, and I didn't intend on changing that. Allies was good enough for me.

"How are things going?" she asked. Right to the chase.

Good. I could appreciate her wanting to keep this as short as possible.

"Badly, overall," I admitted. "Khonsu is here already, and willing to join the cause, but the others are proving a little trickier." That was a nice way of putting Horus being hateful and Amun randomly turning up. "Though I have a lead on where Atum is." Finally.

"That's good. We need him on side almost more than the others," she admitted.

"Oh?" Could I get away with not turning Horus?

"You know who he is..." she started.

"Yes. The creator of all, including himself." At least, that was what he'd claimed to the humans, and they'd believed him. I was skeptical about some of it, but there was no doubt Atum was older, and more powerful, than most of the rest of us. He'd probably only lost a small portion of his magic too. He wasn't as well known in the modern world as me or Ra, but he'd also had more power to begin with.

Ma'at nodded, not feeling the need to explain further. I appreciated that. She clearly recognised that I was intelligent enough to get to the right conclusions without her prodding.

"Several of the others have told me they won't even consider coming over to our side until Atum is here."

"Even with Ra?" My eyebrows knitted together at that. While Atum was powerful, I wouldn't say he was the most influential.

Ma'at grimaced. "Ra's made himself a lot of enemies."

"Ah." I hadn't had much to do with him in the past few thousand years, but I'd heard the rumours. Everyone had. And they hadn't been helped by Sekhmet's return and anger at him. A lot of not very flattering things had ended up being said about him, and I'd heard them all. Which meant others had too.

"And how flexible are you about getting Horus and Amun on board with this?" I asked, hoping she'd say it didn't matter, and that I could stop trying to convince them.

"I'm not," she assured me.

Damn. Just what I'd expected.

"We need all of them, Hathor," she added. "We need as much power as we can get. Seth has turned some of the still powerful gods to his side, who knows what he can do with them."

"Hmm. That is a problem," I admitted, thinking

back to what Anku had said about there being a god among the men who'd destroyed my temple. Of course, that didn't mean anything. Seth could be recruiting demi-gods to worship those of his gods who had lost some of their magic. It wouldn't restore them to full power, but it would do enough. Having some allies he didn't have to do that for would certainly make things easier for him.

"Exactly. And if we don't sway them to our side, then we risk Seth managing to do just that."

I sighed deeply. "No one is going to be allowed to stay neutral, are they?"

"No," she acknowledged. "And not because of me."

"I think it's a little bit because of you," I countered. "Would Seth be doing what he is if you weren't interfering?"

"You know he would be," she insisted.

"No. I know he'd be plotting something. He's Seth, he's always trying to unleash chaos. But people seem to forget that he has two sides to him, like we all do. And one of them isn't bad."

"True, but he doesn't seem to be showing much of that one at the moment," Ma'at supplied.

"Which doesn't mean he won't. So far, Seth has never managed to destroy the world." I wasn't even completely sure that was what he wanted. It wasn't very clear at all. "And there's no reason to believe that this time is going to be any different."

"It *feels* it."

I raised an eyebrow. This wasn't a side of Ma'at that I was used to seeing. She was stubborn.

"Has anyone tried talking to him?" I couldn't believe this was the direction I was going in after he sent people to destroy my temple and scare my priestesses. But when it came down to it, I wanted to protect the most people possible, and an all out war with Seth wasn't going to do that.

"We sent envoys," she said. "Ra himself went. Nothing came of it except an attempt to destroy his retinue."

"Ah." I should have known. Despite what I was saying, I knew that the chaotic side of Seth wasn't one that could be reasoned with. "And what are you planning on doing with him once you've stopped him?"

Ma'at grimaced. "I don't know," she admitted.

"It's probably something you should figure out." Especially as killing him wasn't an option. Not only *couldn't* we do that, but it also wasn't a good idea to. The world needed chaos. Just like it needed all the other things. That was why there was a god of it in the first place.

When she didn't reply, I decided our conversation was over. She hadn't exactly told me anything I didn't already know, but it didn't matter. I had Horus to blackmail, and Amun to convince of something. I wasn't too sure what yet. He didn't seem to be particularly interested in what was going on.

"Where are you going?" Ma'at asked.

"To do what you want me to." I didn't add to my statement, and walked off, ignoring the inviting pools surrounding me. If I liked Ma'at more, perhaps I'd ask to come back here at some point.

As I was approaching the door to the private sanctuary, Maahes appeared. The two of them weren't doing much to hide what was going on between them then. I supposed they could claim to be planning a war, which was partly true, but I doubted it.

"Hathor." He dipped his head in acknowledgement.

"Maahes," I returned. "She's by the fourth pool on the left," I told him.

"Thank you." He slipped past, hurrying towards where the goddess of truth and justice sat.

A pang of jealousy shot through me at the sight. No one wanted me that way. I didn't think I'd wanted them to, but now I was seeing it in front of me like Ma'at and Maahes, I wasn't too sure. Perhaps it *was* something I wanted.

Amun's face swam through my mind, but I pushed it aside. I barely knew him. Other than being physically attracted to him, there was no reason for me to want him. And yet, something about the way he'd acted while in my room made me *want* more.

No. I couldn't think of him right now. Not when I needed to blackmail Horus. That should be my main focus right now. I could work out the complicated emotions I was feeling about someone I didn't know later.

CHAPTER TWELVE

THANKFULLY, Khonsu had been right about Horus not bothering with an amulet to protect against me entering his temple. He probably couldn't put one up without blocking people he wanted to visit him, the moon god included.

I sauntered in, trying to project as much confidence as I could into my movements. It wasn't that hard. The moment I'd become goddess of dance, my body had become fluid and graceful. There was no way to feel insecure in it. Especially when my beauty aspect had been added to it. That one hadn't changed me in the slightest, instead, it had filled me with the knowledge that every person is beautiful in their own unique way, and that flaws didn't hide that beauty. The opposite was true. An imperfection was part of what made someone them, and it gave a chance for their true beauty to shine through.

Not that all the people who had prayed to me for help with their beauty understood that. Most of the time, when someone asked for help with their appearance, all I had to do was gift them a small amount of confidence, and then they shone on their own. It was one of the things I most enjoyed doing, and it was a shame I didn't get to experience it any more. The gods and demis mostly didn't need the help in that department, and hardly any humans asked for mine. And without the requests, there was nothing I could do.

"Your Eminence," Horus' priest said, surprise in his tone. I should learn the man's name if I was going to keep turning up here. It was rude of me to keep thinking of him as the man.

"I'm here to see Horus."

"He said..."

"I know what he'll have said," I cut him off. "But I'm not going to listen to him."

The man sighed, as if he'd known what I was going to say before I had. As I'd noted before, he was smart.

"I'll make my way through," I said.

The priest nodded, no doubt resigned to the

sparring match between two deities he'd managed to get himself caught in.

"You again? I was hoping for someone prettier," Horus drawled from where he was lounging on his throne.

"Unfortunately, Khonsu is busy right now," I said sweetly. "So you'll have to put up with me."

"I told you not to come here again."

"And I decided not to listen. I can be annoying like that."

The expression on his face was impossible to read, even as I got closer to him. Was he more bemused or annoyed? The truth was, I'd probably never find out.

"You're persistent, I'll give you that," he muttered.

"I know what I want, and then I go get it," I informed him. "And right now, I want you to agree to Ma'at's plan."

I was level with his throne now. I could have climbed the platform it was on and stood next to him, but I didn't need to. One thing Horus still had to learn about me was that I didn't take kindly to shows of power that didn't mean anything. Which was *exactly* what he was doing right now.

"I'm not going to do that."

"Why?"

His surprise at my question cut through his carefully configured mask, revealing that hadn't been the question he'd expected me to ask.

"Isn't it your job to protect the people?" I asked.

"The people don't want protecting any more," he responded.

"And that means your job no longer exists? I didn't think that was what it meant to be Pharaoh." I started to pace back and forth, tapping my chin as if I was thinking while I did. I wasn't sure if this line of reasoning was going to get through to him, but I had to hope it would.

"The time of the Pharaohs is long passed." He leaned back in his chair, not seeming to care about anything. "Now is the time for me to relax. You should try it some time, Hathor. It might stop some of those wrinkles from forming."

I snorted. "You're going to resort to telling me I look old?" I couldn't believe what I was hearing. "We both know I don't look a day over twenty-five at the most. Nor do you. Or any of the others. That kind of insult isn't going to work on me."

He crossed his arms and glared at me.

"Besides, I have been relaxing. I've done nothing but enjoy myself for thousands of years. But enough is enough. The people may have forsaken us, but that gives us no excuse. We have the power to protect and serve them, and just because the humans have forgotten us for now, it doesn't mean we don't still have that responsibility. We should be doing our best to save lives despite how the humans act about us."

"Do you actually believe the nonsense you're spouting?" he asked.

"Yes." The word surprised me. At first, I'd thought it was nothing more than an argument I wanted to use to convince him, but now I'd said the words out loud, I realised how true they were. I really *did* feel that way. And a small part of me hated myself for being so complacent for so long.

But self-loathing wouldn't change anything. The best way for me to undo any of the damage I'd done was to move forward and start living by the words I'd said. I had to protect people. That was why I was doing Ma'at's bidding, after all. Simply because a child moved out of their parents home, it didn't stop them being a family. That was the same for the humans of the world. They'd moved on from us. There was no way to deny it, and I wasn't going to try. But that didn't mean I shouldn't still help them if I could.

Once this was over with Seth, I was going to do my best to find ways to help people without them having to ask for it first. One must exist. I just had to figure out the *how*.

"You're deluded, Hathor," Horus shot at me, breaking through my thoughts.

"And so are you," I responded. "Do you really think Seth is going to leave you alone once he's done with the rest of us?"

He shrugged. "I've defeated him before, I'll do it again."

"Yes, you defeated him once. When you were at the height of your power, and he had less of his. But things have changed, Horus. He's spent all of this time recruiting followers and doing what he can to consolidate his power. And what have you done? Nothing but sit on your throne and enjoy life's pleasures."

He scowled at me, but made no move to leave the room. Perhaps he saw the truth in what I was saying after all. It wouldn't matter today. I didn't think there was anything I could say or do to convince him that he needed to join us right now. But when he'd had time to think about it, when he couldn't see my face and be annoyed by my very existence, then perhaps he'd come around.

I sighed dramatically. "I came here to blackmail you," I admitted.

Surprise flitted over his face. "And?"

"I'm not going to bother."

"It wouldn't have worked anyway," he pointed out.

"Maybe it would, maybe it wouldn't. You hate the rumours that we're mother and son. I could have said something to make them worse."

"Which would affect you too," he countered.

"Perhaps. But also, probably not. I'm the goddess of motherhood, remember? Which would probably be *less* weird if I had a child." How was I getting dragged into this again? "But it doesn't matter. I'm not going to do it."

"Why?"

I let an amused smile lift the corners of my lips. "Because you're going to join the cause yourself. You don't know it yet, but the thoughts are already circling your mind. Wouldn't it have been easier to defeat Seth all those years ago with dozens of other gods and goddesses standing behind you? That's what we can offer this time. You don't have to do it alone."

I considered waiting for him to respond, but decided against it. There was very little point when he wasn't going to accept the way things were yet. And I didn't blame him for that. It wasn't as if I'd come around straight away myself. Which made my decision simple. It was time for me to leave and let him think about it.

I spun on my heels, and stalked off back through his temple.

His priest stepped forward as I passed him, but backed off when he saw the determined expression on my face.

I wasn't sure how I knew, but this visit to Horus' temple meant I had two down, and two to go. Those were better odds than I thought they'd be when I'd woken up this morning.

CHAPTER THIRTEEN

"ARE you sure Horus won't mind you being gone this long?" I asked Khonsu between breaths. The mountain was both easier and tougher going than I'd expected, but at least that meant I could talk with my companion.

He chuckled in response. "What's a few days to a god?"

I shrugged. "I wouldn't know. I've never felt the way you two do about one another towards anyone."

"Woah, we don't feel anything. It's just sex."

"Tell that to the look on your face whenever you say his name," I pointed out. "Don't forget I'm..."

"The goddess of love," he finished for me. "It's annoying that you're the goddess of practically everything."

I shrugged. "I can't help it."

"I know. But there has to be *something* you don't know anything about."

"I'm a solar goddess not a lunar one?" I turned down the small dirt path which appeared to spiral up the very tip of the mountain. We should be at Atum's temple within the next fifteen minutes, which was a relief. I didn't like how long it had taken us to get here. Nor how isolating the trek had been. Not when there were so many other things we should be doing back at Karnak.

"Nice try. We both know that doesn't really mean anything."

"Hey, I tried," I protested.

And it really wasn't my fault that I was the goddess of so many things. Humans had done that to me, it wasn't something I'd decided for myself. Though some of them did link together nicely, and I liked that.

"So what *is* going on between you and Horus?" I asked after a few moments of silence.

Khonsu sighed. "Something? Nothing? I couldn't tell you. That god is a closed book that no one can read."

"For what it's worth, I think he likes you."

"How could you possibly know that? He barely gives you the time of day, never mind intimate details about his emotions," Khonsu pointed out.

"You may be right, there. But some things, I can sense. And when I said your name the other day..."

"You said my name while blackmailing him?" Hurt threaded through the man's voice.

"No, I promise I didn't. I mean, I didn't even blackmail him in the end."

"Wait, but wasn't that why you were going in the first place?" he asked.

"It was. And I was ready to do it. But while I was there, I realised he had to come to the decision on his own terms, like I did. It isn't up to me to blackmail anyone. That's not my style anyway."

"Isn't it exactly what Ma'at did to you?" he asked.

"Hmm. Not really. She threatened to blackmail me, but I doubt she'd actually have done it. This agenda of hers has definitely loosened her up, but I don't think she'd compromise herself that way. How would she be able to carry out her job if she did?" Justice was important to her, and she wouldn't betray that to get what she wanted. Which might have made what she did to me an empty threat, but I supposed that didn't particularly matter once I'd decided I was going to do what she wanted anyway.

"But Horus said he'd been thinking about what you said yesterday morning. Before we left," Khonsu mused.

Ah. So that was where he'd been. I had wondered,

but felt like it was rude to ask without the topic being raised by him first.

"I'm glad to hear it," I admitted. "But that wasn't to do with blackmail. I just reminded him of his past battle with Seth, and what our duty to humankind was. I didn't expect him to be responding to it so soon, actually."

"He was distracted all night." Khonsu pouted at that.

I let out a snort, before trying to cover it with a cough. "I'm sorry, I don't mean to laugh. It's just hard to imagine Horus in such a tender moment."

"We can talk about your bedchamber visitors instead," he suggested.

"That would be a very boring conversation," I assured him. "I can't remember the last time I took a lover." Even that had become boring over time, and it would take someone special to change that.

"Then why was there a man's perfume lingering in your chambers when I went to play with Ura?"

"I thought you only liked to play with Horus' snake," I teased.

Khonsu smirked, the amusement shining through his eyes. "And sometimes, I like to play with something smaller."

A wry chuckle escaped me.

Our conversation paused for a moment as we came to a set of stairs carved into the mountain side. There was no denying they would make things easier to climb. I supposed the whole place was designed to be difficult, but not impossible. A temple would only have been set up in order for human worshipers to visit.

"We must be getting close," Khonsu observed as we began to climb.

"Yes." Excitement and nerves warred within me. I was looking forward to potentially convincing another god to join our cause, but at the same time, I'd never stood before anyone as old as Atum before, and I knew it wasn't going to be easy.

"But you still haven't told me who was in your chambers?" he prompted as he held back a stray branch so I could step past.

"Thank you." I took it from him so he could come past without it hitting him too. "And it was Amun. He decided to pay me a visit."

"You found him?" It was impossible to miss the surprise in his voice.

"I think it was more a case of he found me."

"Did you persuade him to join Ma'at's cause?"

Ah. Now there was a loaded question. I hadn't persuaded him at all, but that was mostly because I hadn't even asked yet. I'd been too distracted with the way he made me feel. But somehow, that felt like something I wasn't ready to admit out loud.

"No, not yet," I said. "But I'm working on it." His ankh rested heavily in my pocket, reminding me of what he said. Perhaps after we returned from persuading Atum, I'd call on him, and I'd say what I needed to before I let him get too close.

"That's a shame. If we could have secured Atum today, and had Amun ready, then we'd only have to finish convincing Horus, and your job would be done," he said.

"Hmm." Somehow, I didn't think it was going to be as easy as that.

I was saved from answering when we turned another corner and came face to face with the place we came to visit.

I stopped dead in my tracks at the sight before me. Atum's temple was nothing like I'd expected it to be. It was fairly squat, with the entrance and windows carved into the mountain itself. There was no doubt that it felt right for the god who supposedly created everything. Including himself.

Nature had reclaimed part of the temple, with lush vegetation curling around the statues and giving it a wild look. There wasn't anything like it at sea level. There couldn't be. The monuments there were either too well looked after, or two far away from the Nile for this to happen. But with the cool breeze at the top of the mountain, the plant life had flourished.

I suspected there was something magical about the place. Something Atum had created to give himself some peace. But that didn't detract from the beauty of it.

"Why do I feel like it would be disrespectful to go inside?" Khonsu whispered.

"I don't know, but I get it." The feeling was one which had come over me too. It was probably an old protection spell that still emanated power. The stronger ones could last for thousands of years with ease.

"We could go back, pretend we tried..."

I snorted. "And Ma'at would send me right back." I paused for a moment and considered my options. I really didn't feel like I could step inside, despite knowing I had to. "You don't have to come, if you don't want to, though."

"I do," he countered. "I've come this far. Not going with you for the final part of the journey feels like some kind of betrayal."

I smiled uneasily. "Then let's get this over with."

After taking a steadying breath, I stepped forward and towards the temple. If Horus couldn't scare me away, then I wasn't about to let an old protection spell. Especially when I wasn't doing anything that needed protecting from. I was here to ask for help. Nothing more. I could do this.

Khonsu followed me, with a similar hesitation in his stride. I hoped this wasn't a sign of what was to come once we got inside.

CHAPTER FOURTEEN

THE EMPTINESS of the temple brought an ache to my chest. No wonder no one had heard from Atum in so long, he was suffering from a lack of priests.

We twisted through the corridors, following what seemed like the most likely path to get to the main audience chamber without knowing if it was the right one. I'd never been here before, and I was assuming Khonsu hadn't either from the way he was acting. Which meant that every step of the way was a guess.

"Why aren't there any priests?" Khonsu asked, echoing my thoughts.

"Your guess is as good as mine," I responded. At the moment, my only theory was that Atum must have sent them away for a reason I couldn't work out. Surely he should still want people to attend on him? Even if it was only for the basics like making sure the temple was cleaned.

"Maybe he's so powerful that he doesn't need them any more?"

"I don't think so. He has priests at Karnak, I always see them at the festivals." Which doesn't answer any of the questions I have about this place.

We turn another corner and come into a courtyard with a huge entrance way at the opposite side.

"I guess that's the audience chamber," I said, glancing at Khonsu for confirmation of my theory.

He nodded, which was a good thing. With nothing else to go with, we had to rely on my guess.

The two of us walked forward, neither too fast, or too slow. We didn't want to go in there, but at the same time, we had to. It was a strange feeling, and one I wasn't sure how to process.

The moment we stepped through the stone doorway, I knew we'd made the right decision about what was lying beneath us.

Atum sat on the giant stone throne in the middle of the room, a serious expression on his face. He was larger than life, but it didn't have anything to do with his stature. From what I could tell, he was the same height as any normal god. But his demeanor was something else. There was no doubt in my mind that this man was more powerful than anyone I'd ever met.

"Who are you?" Atum demanded.

I straightened, not having expected that question. I'd been around long enough that most people knew who I was even if they hadn't met me.

"I'm Hathor, Goddess of..."

"I don't care what you're the goddess of," he cut in. "What are you doing here?"

I swallowed down my nerves. This was what I'd come for, and getting straight to the point seemed perfectly reasonable to me, especially when it meant I could get everything over with in one go.

"I've been sent to speak to you about a very important matter."

"Important to who?" His voice boomed and echoed around the room, impossible to ignore, and filled with raw power.

"Ma'at sent me." The words came out shakier than I expected.

Khonsu reached out and placed a comforting hand on the middle of my back. Probably unnoticeable to the god in front of us, but reassuring all the same. I wasn't here alone, and I didn't have to face him without at least some back up.

"She's forming an alliance to combat Seth's growing powers. We believe he means to cause great harm to the world." That was a fair enough explanation. At least, I thought so. Potentially a little simple compared to the true complexities of the situation at hand, but it was easier to approach things that way, and expand once he was already listening.

"That doesn't concern me," Atum said.

"It should." I stepped forward, the desire to do what was right for the humans of the world rising up within me. "If Seth gets his way, then the world will never be the same again."

"You say that as if it's a bad thing." His eyes bored into me, cold and hard.

"Don't you care?" I spat out without meaning to. "You created so much, and you're willing to let it all fall apart because Seth wants chaos?"

"The rise and fall of the world has happened many times over, and will happen many times again. Why should I be concerned about this one?" He barely moved as he spoke, as if he'd been in this one position for so long, that he had no idea how to be in another one.

"You should care because people will die. You should have cared the other times too," I countered. How could someone who deemed himself to be a creator be so callous about the fate of the world? It wasn't right.

Atum rose to his feet and stepped toward me.

Despite myself, I stumbled back, a little intimidated by the way he was moving, even if I tried not to be.

"And why should I care what petty gods and goddesses are doing?" he asked, stalking forward with every word.

I swallowed my fear. Now wasn't the time for it. "We're not petty," I insisted, though now he was saying it, I felt smaller and more insignificant than I had in my entire life, and I had no idea what I could do about it.

"You are to me."

"We have a duty to protect the world," I stammered out, trying to repeat the words I'd said to Horus. If they'd managed to convince him to stop and think, then perhaps they'd work on Atum too.

It was wishful thinking, and I knew it. But I was at a loss for what else I was going to do in this situation.

I cleared my throat, determined to continue. He'd come around to our side, he had to. "What we're doing is for the good of the world. For the gods, demis, and humans that live in it. We want to stop one god from gaining too much power and destroying the beauty that makes up the earth. We want to promote balance and harmony."

"So?" Atum raised an eyebrow.

"As a creator, you should want to protect that more than anyone."

He laughed bitterly. "And who are you to tell me that? The goddess of dance and joy? I remember when you came into being. There was nothing serious about you. And now you're who they send to me? Laughable."

He turned away and headed back to the throne.

Tears pricked at the corners of my eyes, but I ignored them for now. I'd pay the price for that later, but I was determined he wouldn't see me cry because of him.

"You will help us, Atum. Even if it takes me years to convince you. You will come, and you will stop the world from turning into ash and rubble." I wasn't sure where the words came from, but I used up every last part of my energy in saying them.

I turned around and rushed out of the temple, not stopping to check on whether Khonsu was following, or if Atum would respond. I needed to get out of here.

More than that, I needed to get somewhere private. Luckily, there was an oasis I used to visit nearby. I could head there and stay safe away from prying eyes until I'd had some time to compose myself again. That would have to do.

"Hathor?" Khonsu called as we exited the temple and found ourselves back among the trees and plants which graced the mountain.

I ignored him. He might be my friend, but that didn't stop the fact I needed time alone. I was sure he'd understand.

"Go back to Karnak," I called over my shoulder. "I'll meet you there."

I didn't wait for him to respond. Instead, I called on my dancing aspect and used the skills to dodge the small rocks and other tripping hazards which littered the path down the mountain. I wouldn't be harming myself during the journey to the bottom.

About half way down, the tears finally broke free. My vision blurred, swimming and hiding the path from me. That sucked, but I knew it was the only way.

My dress tangled on a branch, and I had to stop to pry it free. I untangled it, but managed to rip the pocket in the process. Amun's ankh fell to the ground in the process.

I bent down to pick it up, smoothing my finger over it to clean off the non-existent dirt. Despite myself, I smiled down at it, before sticking it in my other pocket. The last thing I wanted was to lose the one chance I had at turning him to our side, especially when it looked like my mission today had been a waste of time.

But those were things I could deal with once I'd spent some time alone. Right now, I needed it in order to recharge.

CHAPTER FIFTEEN

THE GODDESS of dance and joy? I remember when you came into being. There was nothing serious about you.

No matter how many times I tried to push them away, Atum's words kept spinning around in my head. The worst thing was that he was right. I was nothing more than a goddess of flippant things that no one cared about. Why had Ma'at even bothered to send me? She should have sent Sekhmet instead. At least she had a fearsome reputation. No one would fail to take her seriously.

I hugged my legs closer to me as I stared out into the small lake which sat at the centre of the oasis. A light breeze came up from it, ruffling my hair and giving me a break from the harsh heat of the dessert I'd walked through to get here. Thankfully, it hadn't been a long walk between the mountain and here, so

I hadn't had to put up with the baking sands for long.

Birds skimmed the surface of the water, diving for fish and insects, feeding themselves and going about their lives as if there was nothing more to worry about in life.

It was as peaceful as I remembered. I had no idea why no one came here, or why some humans hadn't found it and turned it into a settlement. Perhaps it was too close to Atum's mountain, and his protection charms scared them off. I'd never know. But that didn't detract from the beauty. If anything, it only increased it.

"This place is beautiful, isn't it?" a familiar voice said.

I let go of my knees so I could twist around and look at the familiar figure of Amun leaning against a tree.

I scrambled to my feet, not wanting to be on unequal terms with him.

"What are you doing here?"

"You touched the ankh and thought about me." He shrugged. "So I came. That was the whole point."

"Oh." Was there a good way to explain that it had been an accident? No. I didn't think so. Which meant I had to use this opportunity to try and bring him around. It couldn't go worse than my attempt with Atum, so I might as well.

"Have you been crying?" he asked.

"No," I denied, the word slipping out far too quickly to be believable. "Yes. I needed somewhere private, so this is where I came. How did you know I was here?"

He chuckled. "I thought well enough ahead to make part of the enchantment a homing device so I'd know where to find you."

"You had it specially made?" I pulled the ankh from my pocket and turned it over in my hand a couple of times, trying to make out if there was anything unusual about it. Other than whatever enchantment he'd put on it.

"Yes."

"Why an ankh?" The symbol for life was common enough, and often associated with both of us. But that wasn't something unique we shared. Most of the gods and goddesses held ankhs in traditional drawings. Unless they were like Ptah or Osiris and not technically alive in the normal sense of the word.

"It seemed appropriate." He pushed away from the tree and began to move towards me. "What upset you?"

Should I tell him? If he was going to help us, then I supposed he'd find out about Atum eventually.

"I went to visit Atum, and he said some things."

"That was a bad idea," he observed.

"Going to visit him?"

He nodded.

"I had no choice," I admitted. I stuck the ankh back in my pocket, not wanting to lose it in the undergrowth.

A scowl passed over Amun's face, but he smoothed it away within moments. "What did he say to you?"

"That I was nothing more than a petty goddess and no one could ever take me seriously," I muttered under my breath.

To my surprise, Amun's spluttered laughter broke through my embarrassment.

"It's not funny. It's true." I crossed my arms and glared at him, trying to show my displeasure in the most obvious way possible.

"Of course it isn't true. You're one of the most important goddesses who ever existed."

"That's not true at all," I countered.

"Come with me." He held out his hand.

I frowned. Why was he changing the subject so quickly? And what did he have in mind? A large part of me *did* want to take his hand, but was it the wisest thing to do?

Then again, no one was here to judge me. I

reached out and clasped my hand around his. It felt oddly reassuring to hold hands with Amun, as if this was something that was meant to be.

I pushed that thought aside. There was no such thing as soulmates, just people who fit together, and those who didn't. Or perhaps that was something I was telling myself so I didn't dwell on the fact I had no one to share my life with.

He pulled me through the trees and towards the lake. I hadn't gone too close in the past, not knowing whether or not there'd be crocodiles. I knew it was silly of me to be scared of something that couldn't hurt me, but I hated the way their large jaws cracked when they bit down on something, and always envisaged my arm trapped between their white pearly teeth.

"Where are we going?" I asked.

"You'll see." He tugged me down to a small rocky ledge next to the lake, then let go of my hand. He climbed down and hung his legs over the side, then gestured for me to do the same.

I frowned, confused by what he was up to, but going along with it despite that. There was something reassuring about being with him. Like I knew I'd be safe if I stayed near him and didn't think too deeply about anything.

Once I'd settled onto the rocky edge, he shuffled

closer. Our legs were within touching distance of one another, but not quite there. As if both of us knew that at some point, there'd be no going back on the attraction between us. But I wasn't ready for this to become physical. I'd long since grown tired of sex without emotions, and I had no intention of changing my view on it, even for him.

"Look down into the water," he said.

I frowned, but did as he said anyway. The water glittered, and my reflection stared back at me. I still looked beautiful, despite the puffy eyes from crying and the odd twig caught in my hair.

"I don't think I understand," I admitted.

"You think of yourself as nothing more than your aspects. But really, you're more than that. Each part of you adds to the others, it doesn't take from them. You are the goddess of dance and joy, you always have been. And there's a part of you that isn't serious, that likes the good things in life, and those that bring nothing but happiness. But that isn't all you are. You're the goddess of motherhood, which gives you the ability to understand true joy, but also true pain. It makes you protective, and nurturing. And you're the goddess of queens. You'd do anything for your people, whether they demand it of you or not. You understand what it takes to lead, what it means to show compassion. You're all those things, Hathor. And you're more than that too."

I sat in silence, letting his words sink in. Did he really think I was all of that? It made no sense. We hadn't spent any time together.

"You don't even know me," I pointed out.

"Exactly," he countered. "I don't know *you* yet, but I know of you. And that everything I've said and more is true. You're the goddess of all those things, and more. They're parts of you, but they're not you. If Atum is claiming that you're never going to be taken seriously, then he's stuck in the past and hasn't considered that people change over time. They grow."

"You're very astute."

"I had to do something after Waset ceased to be." He shrugged, but I could tell it was to cover up how he was really feeling. "And I do *want* to get to know you."

I chuckled. "Fine, what did you want to know?"

"Why do you have a pet snake?" he asked.

"She was a present from a High Priestess, and she's a magical snake who doesn't die, as far as I'm aware. What else was I supposed to do with her?" Though that didn't sum up my affection for Ura.

"Fair."

"Do you have any pets?"

"No," Amun answered. "I used to have a monkey, but he died and I never really moved past it. An immortal snake would be a definite step up."

"You can visit Ura, until you find one of your own, if you want?" I suggested.

A smile lit up his face. "I'd like that, if that's okay?"

I nodded. "Next question?"

"What's your favourite colour?"

"Turquoise."

"Isn't that a bit on the nose?" he teased.

"You mean because the humans tend to paint me in a red or turquoise dress?" I checked. "I suppose so. But I have no idea which came first. Perhaps I like the colour because it was used for me, or it was used for me because I like it. I've never spent much time thinking about it. What's yours?"

"Beige."

I smothered a laugh. "What?"

"Like yellow-y beige. The colour of the stone and sand. It makes me feel at home," Amun explained.

"I get that. There is something comforting about it."

We carried on our back and forth, talking of everything and nothing at the same time. I had no idea how much time passed, or when I stopped feeling sad over what Atum had said to me. What I did know was that Amun made me feel more comfortable, far more quickly than anyone else ever had. Even Khonsu, though the way I felt towards the two men was vastly different.

As the day turned into night, I found myself shuffling closer to Amun for warmth. He put an arm around me, pulling me closer, but not once did he act like he expected more, even though I could tell he wanted it. The situation was confusing, and beautiful at the same time. And one I would cherish for a long time.

CHAPTER SIXTEEN

I TRIED NOT to skip on my way back into Karnak, but it was hard to keep my elation down. I'd spent longer at the oasis with Amun than I'd intended to, not that it took much when I'd never intended to spend any time with him there at all. But it had meant I was coming back here later than anticipated. I hoped Khonsu had gotten back all right, but I was certain he'd make himself known as soon as he heard I was back. He had been living in my part of the temple, with the intention of moving into his own once his priests had arrived to open it up and make sure everything was in working order.

While most gods had complexes and spaces here, they didn't all keep priests and priestesses handy, and that was the case with Khonsu. And with Amun, come to think of it. If he'd had some here, then it would have been far easier for us to get a message to him in the first place. That hardly mattered now, though. Not when I had an amulet which would call him to me whenever I needed it to.

I entered my part of the temple to find stacks of boxes and clay jugs scattered around, and the shouts of small children filling my ears.

A smile stretched over my face as I realised what it meant, and scanned the room for my High Priestess. The moment I laid eyes on her, I gestured for her to come join me. They must have gotten here while I was dealing with Atum.

"Anku, you've arrived," I announced, a lot more upbeat than I had been the last couple of times I'd seen her.

"We finally got everything moved from the temple to Karnak," she answered.

"Good. And the families?"

"All but one agreed to come. But they have let their daughter stay with her friends. I'm sorry that they're making so much noise..."

"Don't be," I assured her. "This place needed some brightening up, and they're just the people to do it. Have you been made welcome? Gotten settled?"

She nodded. "High Priestess Miane has made us all very welcome. We have lodging close together, and the girls have a dorm room they can all share. It's beautiful, but..."

"It isn't home," I finished sadly. "I assure you, I'll try and get Ptah to start work on the renovations immediately. I don't want you to spend too much time away from it." Guilt flooded through me from my neglect. Instead of writing a letter to Ptah straight away, I'd put Ma'at's mission first.

But now, things were going to change. I'd found a new purpose in my life, and I was going to start treating my people better. Perhaps there would be a way for them to help me spread the word about inner beauty and other important messages to the general people, without anyone having to worship me? I'd work on that. There was no way I was going to go back to being bored and trying to busy myself with trivial things.

"Thank you, Your Eminence. Your help means everything to us."

"My help is what I owe to you," I corrected her. "You're my priestesses, which means you're my responsibility to make safe and happy. I failed in that task, and for that, I'm deeply sorry."

She blinked a couple of times, probably as she tried to process what I was saying. I didn't imagine a lot of deities had apologised to their followers.

"We appreciate your help and support," she said weakly.

"I'm glad. But I've taken up too much of your time. Please, excuse me."

She went back to her various tasks, making sure that each of the boxes got taken to the right place. While some would contain priceless treasures which had survived Seth's attack, and would simply need storing until they could return to the temple they called home, others contained wine and fruits which would need to be added to my general stores so they could be used before they were spoiled.

Which reminded me, I should also write a note to the kitchen and let them know that I had more mouths than before to feed. The last thing I wanted was for my priestesses to go hungry because of an oversight. I'd do it at the same time I wrote to Ptah.

I made my way back into the main temple and headed towards my bedchamber. Dust and sand from the desert still clung to my hair and clothes, and it would be best if I could bathe before I did anything else.

"Hathor, you're back," Khonsu said, rising from his seat behind the *Senet* board.

I was pleased to see High Priestess Miane was soundly beating him. She rose to her feet and dipped her head, before disappearing off to do something that didn't involve eavesdropping. My priestesses were well trained from an early age.

"Yes, I just got back."

"Are you all right?" he asked, looking me up and down, then narrowing his eyes. "What happened?"

"Nothing much." I carried on walking towards my chamber. He'd never had a problem walking into them before, I assumed he wouldn't now, either.

"Then how come when we parted ways, you were crying, and now you look as if you spent all of last night getting laid?"

If I turned around, I was certain he'd have a raised eyebrow and an expectant look on his face as he waited for me to fill him in. But that wasn't going to happen. What had passed between me and Amun was private. At least for now. And especially because I hadn't even remembered to bring up the most important question I had to ask him. For some reason, in his presence, I forgot everything but spending as much time as possible with him.

This was ridiculous. I was acting like a teenager experiencing her first crush. And that wasn't me. I was older than that, for a start, and much more experienced. Though perhaps this was what Amun had meant when he'd said there was a part of me that still felt the joy and beauty in small moments.

I pushed the thought away. It wasn't important right now.

"Well?" Khonsu prompted.

"I didn't sleep with anyone," I assured him. "I went to an oasis and did some soul searching. Now I'm back." None of that was a lie. At no point had I said I was alone when I was doing it.

"Hmm. Somehow, I don't believe you."

I unhooked my collar and slipped it off, putting it back in place on my jewelry stand. My cuffs followed. I rubbed my wrist where one of them had chafed too much thanks to the sand. This was why I hated the desert. Remembering the ankh, I slipped it out of my pocket, being careful to keep my mind blank. I didn't need to summon Amun right now, and it would only serve to feed Khonsu's need for gossip if I did.

"I promise, if I do anything with anyone, you'll be the first to know. Well, the second."

He chuckled. "That's a good point. I don't think I *want* to be the first."

I shook my head in bemusement. "The feeling is mutual."

"But you're okay, right? Nothing bad happened..."

"No. Nothing happened that you need to worry about," I promised. "But I do need a bath. There's sand in places I don't even care to think about."

"We live in Egypt, there's always sand," he quipped.

I flashed him a wry smile. "The priestesses do a fantastic job of keeping it out of the temple, and you know it. Now shoo. I have a bath to get to."

"Your wish is my command." He bowed dramatically, then left my chambers. Hopefully to go find Horus and remove some of his pent up energy.

Now I could focus on getting clean, and writing my letters to Ptah and the kitchens. Once I'd done that, I could start worrying about the rest of the things I had to do, including a new approach on how to persuade Atum to help with Ma'at's cause.

CHAPTER SEVENTEEN

I GESTURED to one of my priestesses, a girl named Titi. She wasn't particularly high up the hierarchy, but that didn't matter. All of them served me because they wanted to, and all of them were more than capable of doing any of the tasks I needed.

"Your Eminence." She dipped her head. "How can I serve you?"

"Can you deliver two letters for me, please?" I asked, holding them out to her.

"Of course. Where would you like them to go?" She took them from me, and held them tightly, as if she would never let them go.

"The top one is for the kitchens, the second is for Ptah. You can give that one to one of his priests, I know they'll get it to him," I assured her.

"Of course, Your Eminence. I'll see to it right away."

"Thank you, Priestess Titi."

Her face lit up at my use of her name, as if me knowing it was everything she'd ever dreamed of. I should make sure my priestesses remembered they were allowed to have lives of their own too. I knew some gods didn't like their servants mixing with others, but I had no problem with it. Especially when it would likely result in some love matches for them. Everyone deserved to find love.

Hmm. I seemed to have become a romantic overnight. Or perhaps it was the newly cleaned skin which was making me feel that way. It was hard to tell.

"Your Eminence?" Miane said.

I turned to face my High Priestess. "Is everything all right?" She wouldn't normally bother me unless something needed my immediate attention.

"Horus is here to see you."

"Me, or Khonsu?" I checked. It was probably the latter. The two of them seemed to have become important to one another particularly quickly. Though they were still in denial about it.

"You, Your Eminence."

I nodded. "Very well. Please clear the audience chamber and set out a jug of our best wine."

"With two goblets?" she asked.

"Make it three." I imagined Khonsu would join us at some point, and it would be rude not to have anything for him. "Send him in as soon as the wine is here."

She nodded, then hurried off to do as I'd instructed, though the audience chamber was already mostly empty. I looked around it, trying to work out where the best place was to sit. He'd always been perched on his throne when I'd gone to see him, but that didn't feel right. It wasn't *me*. I didn't want to wield any power over him. Not in the slightest.

Instead, I pulled up three chairs around the small table which normally housed the *Senet* board when it was being played. Someone must have thought to clear it away, though I had no idea who.

Moments later, one of the priestesses entered, then set down a tray with the wine I'd asked for.

"Thank you," I said softly.

She smiled, but didn't say anything. She must be one of the newer girls, then. Or one who had lived at the temple with Anku who wasn't used to me being around as much. It didn't matter, she'd be gone within a few moments. She excused herself and disappeared.

Horus walked in after a few more minutes, with

Khonsu walking a couple of steps behind him. I was glad I'd guessed that one correctly.

"Welcome," I said. "Take a seat."

I poured the wine into the goblets and waited for the two of them to properly join me.

Horus took a seat, followed by Khonsu, though I couldn't help but notice that the latter shuffled his chair back a bit, as if wanting to distance himself from the conversation. Interesting. So, he either knew what Horus was going to say, and thought I wouldn't like it, or he had no idea at all, and was preparing for the two of us to go crazy at one another. Both of those seemed like reasonable responses.

"I was starting to think you never left your temple," I said.

Horus chortled. "Of course I do. There's plenty of interest beyond the four walls of a bathhouse."

"And yet, that's where you've been holed up for...how long was it?"

"Longer than I have any need of counting."

I smiled and offered him wine. He stared at it suspiciously.

It was all I could do to stop myself from rolling my eyes. "Poison wouldn't even work on you, what are you so worried about?"

"You passing off the bad stuff on me," he answered, a hint of truth in his words.

"That simply isn't possible," I assured him. "I don't *keep* any of the bad stuff in my stores."

"Hmm. I suppose the proof is in the drinking." He took a sip, then met my gaze. "That is good."

"I'm aware." I picked up my own goblet and took a sip.

Khonsu took his own, but only shifted uncomfortably in his chair. "Rus has something to tell you," he prompted the other man.

I raised an eyebrow. They'd come up with adorable names for one another already? Things were progressing faster than I thought for the two gods.

"Oh?" I turned my attention fully to Horus, expecting him to say whatever it was.

"I agree to help you with your plan," he murmured under his breath.

It took a moment for his words to register. They hadn't been anywhere close to what I'd expected him to say, and I wasn't too sure how to process that.

"Come again?" I asked. The last thing I wanted to do was misunderstand what he'd said and the consequences.

"I'm agreeing to help with your plan," he said, louder this time.

"You mean Ma'at's plan," I pointed out.

"Fine. Ma'at's plan. Does it make a difference whose it is?"

I shrugged. "Not really, I suppose. Given there isn't much of one yet other than get the support of as many people as possible," I admitted.

"That doesn't sound like Ma'at."

"No. She's changed a bit. I haven't spent too much time dwelling on it." It's none of my business what the other goddess' exact reasons were, so long as it saved as many people as possible from horrible and painful deaths. "What changed your mind?"

Horus glanced at Khonsu. Hmm. Had he talked the other god around? It was interesting pillow talk if so.

"I thought about what you said, and you were right," Horus admitted softly.

"Say that again?" I wanted to revel in the moment he accepted what I'd said.

"No. I won't. You heard me the first time," he snapped.

"Sorry, you're right. I did." I took a sip of wine, calming myself.

"I still don't like you." He set his goblet down and crossed his arms. "Even if you have good wine."

"I don't particularly like you either," I countered.

"But that doesn't matter if we have one another's backs."

He nodded. "Good. I'm glad that's settled."

I wasn't about to admit it out loud, but it felt sort of anti-climatic to have his ascent to the plan now. Like I'd been building up to some kind of showdown with him, and now nothing.

I shouldn't complain. At least this will keep Ma'at off my back, and I still have Atum to convince, and Amun to ask.

Horus didn't wait for me to say anything, but turned to Khonsu. "Is there anywhere private we can go?" he asked.

"There's my room?" the moon god suggested.

I sighed. "You have your own temple, Horus. How much more private can you get?"

"The priests gossip," he said by way of explanation.

"And I'm sure my priestesses will too." And I wasn't sure why that even mattered when the priests at his other temple were already aware of the situation.

"Let's go , we can figure it out," Horus announced, getting to his feet.

Khonsu shot me a look, as if he wanted to check I was okay with him leaving.

"Go," I mouthed. I wouldn't want to stand

between the two of them. Not when it clearly meant as much as it did to both of them. From what I could gather, they were starting to spend every moment they could together.

I leaned back in my chair, sipping my wine as I watched them go. Soon, my priestesses would want to be back in the room, but for now, I was going to make the most of the quiet.

CHAPTER EIGHTEEN

I SET my goblet down and took a deep breath, closing my eyes. I still couldn't believe what had just happened. Horus had agreed to be part of Ma'at's plan. And I hadn't even had to blackmail him.

"I thought they'd never leave," Amun said.

My eyes widened as he sauntered over, having appeared as if from nowhere. At some point, I was going to have to ask him what gift he had that meant he could do that.

He picked up one of the goblets, and poured wine into it.

"That's my glass," I pointed out.

He grinned wickedly, then slowly brought it up to his mouth. His eyes locked on mine as he took the slowest sip imaginable.

A small shudder rushed down my spine at the

gesture, and I wasn't sure why. Was I *that* into him? I honestly hadn't thought it was possible.

"Were you waiting the whole time?" I asked once I'd been able to compose myself again.

"I've been here since you came out after your bath," he told me. "Don't worry, I didn't watch."

"Hmm." The worst part was, I wouldn't have minded if he had. "Maybe next time." Oops. The words were out before I'd thought about saying them.

Amun winked at me, then came over, pulling the chair Khonsu had been using closer and dropping down into it. Our knees brushed against one another in a move which had to be intentional.

"What are you doing here?" I asked, without a hint of accusation in my voice.

"I wanted to see you."

"You saw me last night," I pointed out.

"True. But after we parted ways, I couldn't stop thinking about talking to you again."

A small laugh escaped me. "Somehow, I don't think it's talking you have in mind."

"Are you trying to suggest that *hasn't* been on yours?" he asked, studying me intently.

"Yes," I admitted. There was no use in lying. I was reasonably certain he could read the direction of my thoughts on my face, and in my raised pulse. "But that doesn't mean I'm going to act on it." *Yet.*

He nodded, as if understanding the unspoken word. "Your company is more than enough." *For now.*

I leaned in, and placed my hand over his where it rested on his leg. I regretted it almost instantly. The touch was far more intimate than I'd expected it to be, and I couldn't take it back. Instead, I stayed as still as possible, hoping it wouldn't spook him.

"It's just that I don't know you well enough," I admitted. It was better to go with the truth, right? If he didn't like it, and decided never to spend any time with me ever again as a result, then that was his problem not mine. If I kept telling myself that, then perhaps I would begin to believe it.

"Did last night not help?"

"It did." I nodded to back up my point. "It was wonderful. But if we include the first time we met, and that's being generous, this is the fourth time in my life that we've spent any time together."

"Ah."

"And given that we're both going to live forever, I'm not ready to rush into something that could prove awkward for both of us further down the line." I'd heard of more than one occasion where a break up between gods had turned sour. I wasn't in any rush for that to be the two of us in a couple of hundred years.

"That's fair."

"Why are you being so nice about this?" I blurted. "Shouldn't you be telling me that it doesn't matter, and that we can do what we want?"

"Is that what you want me to be doing?" Amun asked.

"I don't know," I admitted. "Maybe?"

He sighed, but didn't pull away from me. "I'm not contradicting you, or trying to persuade you to do something you don't want to, because that's not the right thing to do," he answered. "Don't get me wrong, I want you. And I think you want me. And we could rush this by going to your bed right now and having the most explosive night of our lives..."

A small laugh escaped me. "You think rather highly of yourself, there."

"Actually, it was you I was thinking highly of," he corrected. "But you're right. If we do that, then we might ruin the other connection we have formed. I enjoyed last night, not because of the vague promise of something physical, but because I finally feel as if I have someone I can talk to in my life."

My heart skipped a beat. He'd probably practiced the lines on dozens of women over his unnaturally long lifetime, but in that moment, it didn't matter.

He leaned in and tucked a strand of hair behind my ear. His mouth followed, brushing against my cheek in an almost kiss.

My breathing hitched. Was he going to kiss me?

"I'd do anything for you, Hathor." The words brushed against my skin, a promise which would always hold true.

Without waiting for him to make the move, I twisted my neck so I was facing him, and pressed my lips against his.

He kissed me back the same instant, his hand cupping my cheek and deepening the kiss. It was better than I'd imagined, full of promises, and futures. Hidden moments, and passion which simmered just beneath the surface.

In that moment, I could have taken him right then and there on the floor of my audience chamber and not cared about any of the things we'd been talking about.

Which was when he pulled back.

A small whimper escaped without me meaning it to, and I bit my lip as I looked up at him.

"Please don't look at me like that, Hathor," he whispered, his voice hoarse and full of promise. "My restraint is holding on by a thread."

I nodded, not trusting myself to speak. If I did, I was certain I'd find myself begging for him to ignore all of my apprehensions and come to bed with me. But no. That wasn't the right thing to do. We needed to learn more about one another, spend time experiencing the things that made us unique.

Then, and only then, could there be more between us.

"I promise, it'll be worth it," he said, leaning in to kiss me gently. He was gone before either of us had a chance to get too caught up in one another.

"I hope you're right. Does this mean you're going to be spending more time in Karnak?" I asked. He had a temple space here that he could use, even if there was no one in it at the moment.

He shook his head. "I'll only be here to visit you," he said.

"Oh." Should I be disappointed or not about that? I supposed it depended how things went.

A knock sounded on the door, stopping our conversation from going anywhere further.

"I need to go," he said. "I'm sorry, and I'll see you soon." He leaned in and brushed another kiss against my lips, before darting off in another direction.

I frowned, a little confused by what had just happened, but mostly pleased. We were on the same page. That was a good thing. It meant I wasn't about to get my heart broken by thinking he was more interested than he was.

CHAPTER NINETEEN

MA'AT STRODE in only seconds after Amun had left. I wasn't sure if that was purposeful on his part or not. But it was definitely bad timing on hers.

I gestured for the priestess on the door, and asked her to fetch another goblet for the wine. It was clear Ma'at had something important she wanted to talk about, or she wouldn't have come here. She wasn't exactly known for her social calls.

Once I had the clean goblet, and the room was empty apart from ourselves, I turned my attention to the other goddess.

"What can I do for you?" I asked.

"I need to know what you said to Atum," she said bluntly.

"Umm. Not much. He didn't seem impressed that I'd been sent as a messenger." And that was putting it lightly. I'd actually have considered his reaction to be bordering on severely insulted, but I wasn't sure that was what Ma'at wanted to hear.

"Well, whatever you said, it's worked."

"What?" I regretted the bluntness of my response the moment it left my mouth, but it was the honest one. Atum hadn't seemed to be in the slightest bit impressed with anything I'd said to him.

"We've sent him countless letters and missives, and Ra even tried to visit. Every one of them was sent back unopened, and Ra was sent away without an audience," Ma'at said.

"And you didn't think to tell me any of that *before* you sent me to go deal with him?" Hurt panged through me. Did she think of me as a petty goddess with nothing serious to offer too?

No. She wouldn't. Ma'at was too involved in the politics of temple life for that one. Plus, she'd come to me for help in the first place, and it wasn't because she'd thought I wasn't worth anything. I had to remember that.

"It didn't cross my mind that I should. I didn't want to influence the way you tried to convince any of them to join the cause."

"Right."

"Anyway. Today, I got a letter from Atum." She picked up her goblet and took a sip.

I downed my own, hoping it would steady my nerves, even though wine had very little effect on me in the first place. I refilled my goblet anyway, and drank some more.

"He's agreed to help with our campaign against Seth."

"He's agreed?" I couldn't believe it. This was the last thing I'd expected to happen after my disastrous run in with the creator.

Ma'at nodded, unable to contain the joy on her face. "He's put some caveats in place, though. He refuses to get involved in a physical war, and won't use magic or powers against any one god. But he will offer advice in strategy and in other ways that could be of use."

"Wow." I leaned back in my chair, trying to process everything she was saying.

Atum was on our side. He'd responded to me.

I didn't want to question the why too closely, especially as none of what had happened up on the mountain made any sense. Perhaps I'd ask Khonsu later. He might have noticed something I didn't.

"Which means we have two of your consorts..."

"Still not my consorts," I corrected her, not even bothering to point out that one of them thought I wasn't worth his time, and two of the others were more interested in one another, than in me. The one left over though...he was another matter. Perhaps in time he *could* become a consort of mine.

"Sorry. I mean the gods you were assigned to..." She waited for me to protest that one.

I still wasn't too keen on the phrasing, but it was better than the alternative, so I let her have that one.

"Two are on our side already, which just leaves Horus and Amun. Any update on them?" she asked.

"Actually..." I took a deep breath. "We have all four of them. Horus came to me about an hour ago to say he'd agreed to be part of whatever plan you have."

"And Amun? I didn't even realise you'd found him."

"I haven't, as such. He found me. I still have no idea where he's been." Or where he was now. But I figured it was better to keep quiet about that particular part of the situation. All she needed to know was that Amun was on our side.

Though I had to admit, that was an assumption. But he'd promised to do anything for me, and that would include going along with Ma'at's plan, wouldn't it?

"All four of them?" Ma'at whispered, but I didn't think I was supposed to actually answer the question. She was just processing it for herself. "I can't believe it. That's amazing."

"You're welcome," I muttered, doubting she was

even aware that I was still in the room right now. I had no idea what was going around the other goddess' head, but it had nothing to do with me.

"We should have a banquet," she murmured.

"What do we need a banquet for?" I asked despite myself.

"For the other gods," she told me impatiently. "Now we have the names we need on board, we need to spread the word so others join us too. We need as many people as possible in order to get this working."

"Oh, right. Is there anything you want me to do?" I asked, feeling like I should.

She shook her head. "Unless you happen to have a dozen spare priestesses, there isn't much you can do," she countered.

"Actually, I do. One of my temples was destroyed by Seth and the priestesses are here. I haven't assigned them any work yet..."

"Excellent. If you send them to my rooms and get them to ask for Edrice, I'll set them to work on the banquet. You'll invite Horus, Khonsu, and Amun, naturally?" she checked. I liked that she assumed Atum wouldn't respond again. It seemed accurate. If I was honest, I didn't expect to see the creator god ever again.

"I will. Though I might not be able to get hold of Amun."

She waved my concern away. "With the other three on board, it'll be enough." She rose to her feet. "Thank you for the wine. It was delicious."

I smiled in acknowledgement, glad my stash of the drink was pleasing so many people today.

"I'll send the priestesses over to you," I promised.

"Thank you." She nodded to me once, then slipped through the door and back out into the main temple.

I leaned back in my chair, satisfied that despite the odds, I'd completed the quest Ma'at had set.

EPILOGUE

THERE WERE FAR TOO many people here for my liking, but it would be cruel to have sent my priestesses to serve at the banquet and then not turn up myself, especially when I was part of the reason Ma'at had managed to achieve her goal in the first place and was able to talk some of the other gods into taking sides. Though I suspected a few of those gathered here tonight might end up defecting to Seth's side. I doubted everyone would agree with us.

Everyone was drinking more than they should and chattering among themselves, while none of them paid much attention to me. I suspected it was because most of them had no idea what role I'd played in making all of this possible, and that was fine by me. I didn't need the attention it would bring me.

I scanned the room, looking for familiar faces and spying relatively few. Of course, I knew most of the gods and goddesses in passing, it was almost impossible not to when we lived in such a small space. But the number of them that I'd refer to as friends was small. I should do something to change that now we were going to be working together.

Khonsu and Horus were sitting next to one another at the opposite side of the hall, eating off the same plate and generally being sickeningly sweet. Apparently, their relationship was out in the open now, then.

Ma'at was busy talking with Isis and her husband, though I wouldn't have called her a friend anyway. Trusted ally was about as far as I was willing to go when it came to the goddess of truth.

Ptah sat talking with his ex-consort and their son, Maahes. It was surprising he wasn't shadowing Ma'at, but perhaps they were still being quiet about their relationship. I pushed thoughts of the two of them aside. They hardly mattered until it came to actually planning the attack on Seth. But I needed to talk to Ptah later. I'd only sent him word about my temple a couple of days ago, so it was too early for me to expect a reply, but a little small talk wouldn't hurt if I ran into him later in the evening.

My gaze reached the end of the long banquet

table, and my heart sank. It was only then that I realised who I'd been looking for. Despite not having seen him since our kiss, I'd been hoping Amun would come. I wanted to spend more time with him, especially because it would give us a chance to get to know one another better and eventually move on to the physical part of our relationship.

I sighed and sank back in my chair, catching sight of the person sitting next to me.

My eyes widened as I recognised the goddess. Nephthys. The last person I expected to see at a banquet for the express purpose of bringing down the reign of her consort. Or probably ex-consort, given she was here.

"I hear you're to thank for the gods agreeing to be part of this," she said to me.

"Only four," I muttered. "Though one didn't take much convincing."

"That doesn't surprise me. Ma'at probably realised she could catch more flies with honey than with vinegar."

I frowned. "What do you mean?"

"Ma'at only does things that suit her," Nephthys said.

"Ah, right. Yes, I've always assumed so." And it didn't bother me for the most part. She was trying to do the right thing, and while I might question some of her execution, I wasn't going to fault her motives.

"All I meant was that her personality can be a bit, prickly sometimes. So she decided to use you in order to persuade people who needed a gentler touch."

"Ah. Yes. Well I don't think Horus would agree to you on that one." Prickly didn't even begin to describe the complicated relationship between us. "But I'm sure Amun would."

She frowned. "Amun?"

"Yes."

"Hathor, Amun is with Seth," Nephthys said.

"No, he isn't. He said..."

"I promise. He's on Seth's side. I was there the day he arrived at Seth's compound and he swore his loyalty to him." The earnestness in her voice made it impossible to ignore what she was saying.

"But, that can't be right." The whole room began to spin as the truth sunk in.

We'd kissed. And I'd told Ma'at he was on our side. But all that time, he'd been aligned with Seth. He might have even been the god who helped destroy my temple.

Love, hate, and anger warred for dominance inside me, and I wasn't sure which of them would win out.

* * *

The End

* * *

Thank you for reading *Quest Of The Goddess*, I hope you enjoyed the first part of Hathor's story. It continues in *Trust Of The Goddess* which will follow what happens next as she sorts out her feelings for Amun, and prepares to take on Seth: http://books2read.com/trustofthegoddess
You can also read First Meeting for free, a bonus scene where Amun and Hathor meet for the first time: https://dl.bookfunnel.com/fsd2vpwn84

AUTHOR NOTE

Thank you for reading *Quest Of The Goddess*, I hope you've enjoyed reading it as much as I have writing it, and will join me again for *Trust Of The Goddess* and *Heart Of The Goddess*. If you want more stories from the world, there is also a series of standalones connected to it, *Protectors Of Poison* follows Serquet, *Daughter Of The Sun* follows Sekhmet, and *Servant Of Chaos* follows Rhodopis (who isn't a goddess directly from mythology, but is from an Ancient Egyptian legend with similarities to Cinderella). There's also a short story following Edrice (Ma'at's priestess) called *Priestess Of Truth*. In the future there will also be a series based on Ma'at and Maahes.

All of the gods and goddesses mentioned (with the exception of Rhodopis) are real ones from Ancient Egyptian mythology. A lot of the ones in this story are major ones too. I have taken some liberties with aspects of them, and their personalities, but have tried to stay as faithful as possible in a lot of aspects of the book. Ancient Egyptian history and mythology has been a passion of mine since I was a child and my Dad showed me *The Mummy* (*1999*) well before he should have (I was only seven when it came out), so much so, that I'm currently fulfilling a lifelong dream of mine and studying for a diploma in Egyptology. I hope this comes across in my writing, as I love the characters so much.

I also want to thank you for sticking with me. Hathor's story changed significantly from what I originally had planned, but the original plot didn't feel right when I was working on the book. It's important to me to tell the story the way it's supposed to be told, and that's what happened with this series. The way it has unfolded feels right to me, and I look forward to exploring the characters more in the next book!

Thank you for reading, and I hope you and your loved ones are staying safe and healthy!

Books in the Paranormal Council Universe

- The Paranormal Council Series (shifter romance, completed series)
- The Fae Queen Of Winter Trilogy (paranormal/fantasy)
- Spring Fae Duology (paranormal/fantasy)
- Thornheart Coven Series (witch romance)
- Return Of The Fae Series (paranormal post-apocalyptic, completed series)
- Paranormal Criminal Investigations Series (urban fantasy mystery)
- MatchMater Paranormal Dating App Series (paranormal romance, completed series)
- The Necromancer Council Trilogy (urban fantasy)
- Standalone Stories From the Paranormal Council Universe

Books in the Obscure World

- Ashryn Barker Trilogy (urban fantasy,

completed series)

- Grimalkin Academy: Kittens Series (paranormal academy, completed series)
- Grimalkin Academy: Catacombs Trilogy (paranormal academy, completed series)
- City Of Blood Trilogy (urban fantasy)
- Grimalkin Academy: Stakes Trilogy (paranormal academy)
- The Harpy Bounty Hunter Trilogy (urban fantasy)
- Bite Of The Past (paranormal romance)
- Sabre Woods Academy (paranormal academy)

Books in the Forgotten Gods World

- The Queen of Gods Trilogy (paranormal/mythology romance)
- Forgotten Gods Series (paranormal/mythology romance, completed series)

The Grimm World

- Grimm Academy Series (fairy tale academy)
- Fate Of The Crown Duology (Arthurian

Academy)
- Once Upon An Academy Series (Fairy Tale Academy)

Other Series

- Untold Tales Series (urban fantasy fairy tales)
- The Dragon Duels Trilogy (urban fantasy dystopia)
- ME Contemporary Standalones (contemporary romance)
- Standalones
- Seven Wardens, co-written with Skye MacKinnon (paranormal/fantasy romance, completed series)
- The Firehouse Feline, co-written with Lacey Carter Andersen & L.A. Boruff (paranormal/urban fantasy romance)
- Kingdom Of Fairytales Snow White, co-written with J.A. Armitage (fantasy fairy tale)

Twin Souls Universe

- Twin Souls Trilogy, co-written with

Arizona Tape (paranormal romance, completed series)

- Dragon Soul Series, co-written with Arizona Tape (paranormal romance, completed series)
- The Renegade Dragons Trilogy, co-written with Arizona Tape (paranormal romance, completed series)
- The Vampire Detective Trilogy, co-written with Arizona Tape (urban fantasy mystery, completed series)
- Amethyst's Wand Shop Mysteries Series, co-written with Arizona Tape (urban fantasy)

Mountain Shifters Universe

- Valentine Pride Trilogy, co-written with L.A. Boruff (paranormal shifter romance, completed series)
- Magic and Metaphysics Academy Trilogy, co-written with L.A. Boruff (paranormal academy, completed series)
- Mountain Shifters Standalones, co-written with L.A. Boruff (paranormal romance)

Audiobooks: www.authorlauragreenwood.co.
uk/p/audio.html

Laura is a USA Today Bestselling Author of paranormal and fantasy romance. When she's not writing, she can be found drinking ridiculous amounts of tea, trying to resist French Macaroons, and watching the Pitch Perfect trilogy for the hundredth time (at least!)

FOLLOW THE AUTHOR

- Website: www.authorlauragreenwood.co.uk
- Mailing List: www.authorlauragreenwood.co.uk/p/mailing-list-sign-up.html
- Facebook Group: http://facebook.com/groups/theparanormalcouncil
- Facebook Page: http://facebook.com/authorlauragreenwood
- Bookbub: www.bookbub.com/authors/laura-greenwood

- Instagram: www. instagram.com/authorlauragreenwood
- Twitter: www.twitter.com/lauramg_tdir